ISHITA AGARWAL was born in Panchkula and has lived in a number of cities before returning close to her birthplace, Chandigarh, where she is currently studying. She spends her free time reading, playing the guitar and blasting away the bad guys in MarioKart and Legend of Zelda on her Nintendo Wii. If she could choose to be gifted with one superpower, it would be flying, as she would rather soar in the open sky than in a claustrophobic aeroplane. Apart from closed flying contraptions, she is terrified of dogs.

Her writing influences include John Green, Meg Cabot and Louise Rennison. She hopes that, in the years to come, Indian teenagers will have access to a wider range of books they can identify with.

Lieable is Ishita's first published work.

LIEABLE

Ishita Agarwal

OM
Om Books International

First published in 2013 by

OM

Om Books International

Corporate & Editorial Office
A-12, Sector 64, Noida 201 301
Uttar Pradesh, India
Phone: +91 120 477 4100
Email: editorial@ombooks.com
Website: www.ombooksinternational.com

Sales Office
4379/4B, Prakash House, Ansari Road
Darya Ganj, New Delhi 110 002, India
Phone: +91 11 2326 3363, 2326 5303
Fax: +91 11 2327 8091
Email: sales@ombooks.com
Website: www.ombooks.com

ISBN: 978-93-83202-35-5

10 9 8 7 6 5 4 3 2 1

Printed in India

Acknowledgements

For my writing journey, which began six years ago, the publication of *Lieable* marks a milestone for me;

My 4th grade teacher, Kimberly Schafer, made me realise that writing can be a lot of fun. Thank you ma'am;

My parents, the rest of my family, especially my little brother, were always encouraging and supportive through this creative journey. Thank you all for being there;

All the students with whom I attend school, particularly my friends (you know who you all are), thank you for providing me endless ideas;

My wonderful editor, Shreya Chakravertty, who helped me shape the book, and my publisher, Ajay Mago, Om Books International, thank you for encouraging a young author like me;

And finally, thank you, dear readers for picking up *Lieable*.

Happy Blah-day to Me 1

I woke up. My Timex was next to the pillow. Crap. Late again. It was the first day of school after the summer vacation.

Then, I remembered. Wasn't it the seventh today? It was July 7. My 13th birthday.

Which meant I could create a legal YouTube account.

Which meant I could create an authorised Facebook account.

Which meant I could do *anything*. Well, not really anything because…um…you get my drift.

I dragged my lazy butt to the bathroom. After I got dressed for school, Dad wished me a happy birthday and presented me a cake (which tasted better than the vanilla cake he had made me last year). Then, he dropped me to school.

I entered the building, not thrilled at all. Oh well, it was better than staying home and getting bored. When I was in my house, there were two sentences I spoke every hour, at the very least. 'Dad, I'm getting bored. What should I do?' If he was at his office, I would call him up and pester him so much, he had to hang up.

'Hey, Janya.'

A voice brought me back to the present as the cacophony around me carried on. My class, 8-B, was the noisiest in the whole school. The teachers kept blabbing on about how bad we were, how no one stopped talking, how everyone cheated during tests. But it was the funniest class in the world, at least according to us students.

'Janya...!'

'What?' I asked, my mind clinging to my thoughts like water to a sponge. They were all around me. I couldn't escape them (my thoughts, I mean).

'It's me, Maya.'

That high-pitched, tone-deaf, blabbermouth of a toad.

'Maya, look at you. What happened?' I was forced to say after looking at her, to continue a conversation I didn't want to have at all. I didn't even want to put an exclamation mark in my voice.

'I just got really, really tanned over the summer,' boasted Maya, trying to work up the fake American accent she 'caught' last winter from her 'cousin'.

'Wow. You look like a baked potato...,' I muttered.

'Did you say something?' she asked. 'Oh, and happy birthday.'

Why, *why* did my birthday always happen to be on the first day of school?

'Um…thanks,' I said, trying not to sound utterly depressed, like Bella Swan from the *Twilight* series. Great. Just great. My first birthday wish (excluding family) was from my super enemend, Maya (we were less friends and more enemies, so 'enemend' fits better than the regular 'frenemy').

'Okay, then,' she said, and happily skipped over to another group of people to, I guess, boast some more.

She was a tall girl, a show-off, the stereotypical mean blond (without the blond hair, of course. Although

I suppose that was just the kind of dumb look she would want). She always tried to compete with me, but everyone knew how dull she was. Everyone *except* her and her joke of a best friend, Annika, who had a face like a horse (really). Maya behaved like she was put on this earth to outdo me at everything.

Unfortunately, she happened to be in my class.

After that unpleasant encounter, I spotted Aditi and Sanchi—my good friends—and went over to talk to them. They were the kind who scored really awesome marks in everything. It wasn't as if I *didn't* get good grades, it was just that...they always did better. But, of all the people in school that I had known over the years, they were the only ones who kind of touched the line of 'normal'. They wished me too, and then began talking about lame Indian TV shows. I can't believe they *liked* those shows. WOW.

'Ma'am is coming!' Dev warned us all, and in the blink of an eye, the chaos of the class transformed into pin-drop silence.

'Good morning, ma'am,' sang the students. I sat down.

Our class teacher Mrs. Miglani was going to assign new partners today since it was the first day after the holidays. I thought back to all the free time I had when there was no school for two months. Now it felt like all I did then was swim and waste my time reading the *Twilight* series. And I didn't grow an inch despite all the time I spent in the water. I was still the olive-coloured, 5-foot 1-inch girl with almost-black eyes and black-brown hair. Oh, and as for *Twilight*? Don't even *ask*.

'Good morning class, sit down, please,' said Mrs. Miglani.

We all hurried back to our seats. 'I hope you had a nice time in the break. We are happy to have you all back.' There wasn't even a hint of excitement in her voice. 'Anyway, a new student is going to join our class from today.'

She gestured towards a boy who came up to the front of the class and introduced himself. I would have been terrified had I been in his place. Having 35 pairs of eyes fixed on you can make you pass out.

'Uh...um...my name is Sameer, and I just moved here from Bangalore...,' he trailed off as he was interrupted by an announcement on the intercom. I could see the relief on his face. Aw, that's so...likeable. His school uniform looked SO good on him. It made all the other boys in our class look like donkeys.

'Nice to have you here, Sameer. Now, first things first. I will be assigning you your new partners,' said Mrs. Miglani. Everyone groaned. I awaited my turn, and according to some kind of crazy seating schedule (which wasn't altered by God in any way, I swear), I was assigned a seat right next to Sameer.

Maya-vitis Syndrome 2

'Hello.'

Oh, man, I could be SO lucky sometimes.

'Um, hi...?' repeated Sameer. He was just *cute.* Nothing else. You know, I didn't *like* him. I was just euphoric over the fact that I didn't have to sit with SBLTOISWBTSH (Some Boy Like the One I Sat With Before the Summer Holidays, DUH!).

'Oh, hey.' There was a part of my mind which was happily dancing away, and another part was just wishing I didn't do anything drastically embarrassing and get the reputation of being a complete weirdo.

'So...uh...you're my partner, huh?' he asked.

Honestly, it was a stupid question. I mean, wasn't it totally obvious if I was sitting on the damn chair next to him? But I forgave him. I didn't want to do anything except giggle like crazy as he looked practically like a Greek god.

'I guess so,' I said, stupidly.

Of course, Aditi and Sanchi were assigned seats close to each other. 'Well…uh…happy birthday,' he said. Oh My God. Did he just wish me?!

'Thanks...uhh...,' I mustered up enough courage to ask, 'How did you know it's today?'

'Your, um, *friend* was talking to you at the top of her voice, so it was not really easy to ignore.'

Maya was too loud, sometimes.

'By the way, she DOES look like a baked potato,' he added with a smile. I thought I felt my heart skip a beat.

This was the best birthday *ever* (even though I wasn't having a party)! I had never been wished 'happy birthday' by a complete stranger and, in this case, a stranger who happened to look better than more than 99 per cent of the school.

After a long wait, the bell for recess finally rang. I sprang out of my seat and bolted for the door. I felt suffocated in that classroom.

'Oh my god! Did you see that Sameer guy? He is so cute! I'm going to try talking to him after school. What d'ya think? And, oh god, he's sitting with you,' Maya exclaimed as we walked down the crowded stairs. I had seen jealousy flaming in her eyes like hot tamale when I kept my schoolbag next to Sameer's. I had thrown a quick glance at her then (oh yeah, I'm evil. If this was a movie, my evil laugh would echo in the background).

But enough about boys. When I was in Class 1, our teacher had asked us if there was anything we were allergic to. I had raised my hand and said that I was allergic to boys. All the girls had cracked up.

'Uh...yeah,' I mumbled, wanting to break Maya's face, and maybe reassemble it a bit too. Her nose should be on her head, her mouth in the place of her eyes (she talked too much) and her eyes in the place of her mouth (she refused to see the real world properly).

'Let's go to the canteen,' she said as she held my hand, leading me to the 'Self-Service Restaurant'.That's what it was called. The world was getting dumber and dumber, day by day.

I grimaced as she took my hand. See, I hated it when people did that. It...it gave me a weird vibe in my brain, setting off an alarm, like I was having an electric shock or something. My palms got all sweaty (like they did during my unit tests, when they were so clammy that the question paper got wet).

'So...what did you do over the summer?' Maya asked.

'Well...I...'

'I'll tell you what I did! I went to my dad's private island near Sicily, you know, in the Mediterranean, and got nice and tanned there! We went snorkelling and scuba diving almost every day! And then we cooled off in the Alps in Switzerland!' she jabbered away.

She was *so dumb*. She couldn't even pronounce Mediterranean properly! It sounded like a disease the way she said it (well, she was a disease herself...maybe it could be called Maya-vitis Syndrome. And if someone caught this incurable illness, they wouldn't ever heal and would most likely turn into a toad for the rest of their lives. It would be worse than AIDS or malaria).

I really couldn't compete with her *grand* holiday now, could I? So I decided to stall for time.

'That's awesome.'

'What did you do?'

Shoot. I was not good at stalling. 'Uh...I went snorkelling too! Then...uh…we went to Canada, and *ohmygosh* there were so many adorable polar bears out there,' I lied. Um...although I didn't think a combination of snorkelling and polar bears could be found in the same place. What if Maya noticed?

'Cool! I did that too, last winter! What do you want to eat?' asked Maya. She was so stupid that she didn't notice my expression as we got closer to the food. I *hated* canteen stuff. But I had to pretend I loved it, or else I would have to eat alone. Seriously.

We got some noodles. I personally thought our school's noodles smelt like poo. And the pizzas...don't even ASK about the pizzas. They tasted like someone had dipped them in petrol before serving us. But, weirdly enough, everyone liked them. Or maybe my taste buds were just dysfunctional.

Then we sat down on a bench and started eating. Well, only her, I guess. I threw my cup of noodles in the dustbin right next to me when she wasn't looking. Sorry, Haiti. I had no choice when faced with the alternative: ingesting the food.

I wanted Aditi and Sanchi to save me. I was only hanging out with Maya because I didn't want to be alone during recess (on second thought, maybe being alone was a better idea after all). But they were nowhere to be seen, probably caught up in some contest. They were the kind of people who always participated in every event and managed to score good marks at the same time. I wondered how they managed to deal with all of that. Plus, Sanchi even had a *boyfriend*.

So much better than me, the incompetent awkward girl.

Really, Dad? 3

At last, the bell rang. I was longing for the day to end so I could go home and hide in my cave (which other people called my room). I nearly raced out of the grounds, past the parked school buses. Almost everyone at my school took the bus to go home. But I was one of the 14 people (yes, I counted. Got a problem with that?) who went home by car or some other private means of transport.

My mom died when I was just one month old (actually it should be 'young' not 'old', because you couldn't be 'old' just a month into your life, but whatever. It was freaky English; that's what my Hindi teacher said), so Dad had always been a bit overprotective.

I missed her. I didn't have any real memories of how she looked, though I had seen her pictures. She looked beautiful. She had short brown-black hair, just a little different from mine. Her hair was straight. Deep down, I knew she was still around, protecting me. But whatever. It's alright, I guess.

Dad was the Managing Director of a company which designs phone applications, so I had enough money to own many iPhones. Not that I did. But he was also an awesome father, not just a moneyman. He always helped me with my Math homework (I was hopeless at Algebra) and also with History and all. Even though he was very busy managing work through his iPhone and two BlackBerry handsets, he always found time for me. I mean, my mom died when I was one month young! Actually, sometimes I didn't really feel that sad about it either. I mean, what was the point? Was it possible to miss something you never knew?

The next day, after reaching class, I plonked myself down right next to the window. I remembered the last time I sat here was with TWB (That Weirdo Boy), before the summer vacations. Just as I was remembering those 'Good Old Times', someone threw their bag on the seat next to mine. What? Oh...Sameer was my partner, so *of course* he would sit with me. I couldn't believe I had forgotten about him. I was so busy thinking about how happy I was back then (back then refers to seventh grade... good times, good times).

'Hey,' I said. I had to say *something*. Otherwise he would think I was one of those girls who kept giggling all the time and were boy-crazy. I was not a giggler. I didn't understand the concept of giggling either. But again, whatever. No reply. I looked to my left. I only saw thin air.

I saw Aditi and Sanchi talking to each other. I went up to them and tried to chime into their conversation.

'So, did you watch that TV show last night?' That was Smitha, a quiet girl who had started hanging out with them because Aditi had supposedly taken a liking to her.

'Oh, no. I was too busy talking to Zayn. You know, he gifted me a teddy bear and a really expensive watch from Archies,' beamed Sanchi. Was she showing off or was it just me who thought so?

'Oh, really?' Aditi asked, not looking that keen to know the rest of her story. She never liked Zayn. Neither did I.

He always seemed a bit of a show-off to me, like Sanchi was. Maybe that's why they liked each other. Although I doubt he really liked her. Whatever. I mean, we all were 13-and 14-year-olds, for God's sake!

'Yes, and you know, we even went out for a movie,' added Sanchi.

Aditi and Smitha gasped.

'Did you take permission from your mom?'

'Oh yeah. She's very cool about him. He even met her once. No fights. He really, really loves me.'

Then…BZZT!!!!

I felt this electric shock inside me as soon as she completed her sentence.

It then became a little itch in my gut. Was I twitching?

'Ouch!' I jumped a step back.

'Yeah, maybe you should get a boyfriend, Janya.' Sanchi said, eyeing me.

'Um…,' I said, tuning myself out of their conversation.

No, how could my stomach twitch? I felt like throwing up.

What was going on? Why did I feel like I was going to explode? Strange.

They carried on, and I was just sitting awkwardly, listening to their conversation and getting bored to death. I was feeling out of sorts, as if there was a hamster running on a wheel inside me, so I excused myself from their chatter. I thought about that nerve-jangling feeling I got a few minutes ago but I just couldn't come up with any explanation for it. I felt uneasy. Maybe these people around me were driving me insane. I was in dire need of new friends.

~

A really life-changing thing happened in Science period that day (for suffering students like us, it *was* a life-changing event). We were all getting bored out of our minds, studying about acids (I mean, who cared about the pronunciation of phenolphthalein? And WHAT did it have to with being a lawyer? Yeah, I wanted to be a lawyer. I was *so good* at fighting and proving others wrong! At least, that's what I thought. I hadn't told anyone about this crazy ambition of mine). Then, one of those orange bees that were really common in the peak of summer came in from one of the office-like windows and into our room. It started circling Ms. Anita's head, and she began swatting at it like it was nothing, like it was just a fly. A bee differed from a housefly in indefinite ways. Flies didn't bite. Bees did.

Apparently, my 'oh-so-smart' Science teacher didn't know this, and the next thing we knew, she had screamed *so loud* that our floor-in-charge and Mr. Gupta, the Math teacher, came bustling into the room and yelled, 'What is GOING ON?'

The Science teacher's face got all puffy and she started emanating wheezing sounds. It was quite an interesting sight. Then, one or two teachers from the other sections also rushed into our classroom—half-running, half-walking. It turned out that Ms. Anita was allergic to bee bites. Well, at least the students were happy. *No more Science* (at least for a week because she had to be hospitalised. I wondered who would visit her, she wasn't even married—yeah, we knew *that much* about our teachers).

~

I had another 'surprise' waiting for me even after school.

'Hi, Janya. I hope you had a nice sports period today,' said Dad on the way home, as he removed the newspapers from where I sat in our Volkswagen (Dad always forgot to put them in the little pocket behind the car seat).

I was sweating like a wild dog, and I could feel that my face was red. 'Meh,' I mumbled. I just wanted to lie motionless.

He stopped at the traffic signal when it turned red. I just wanted the light to remain red forever and never change to green. I didn't want to get out of the air-conditioned car. The AC was on full blast.

Dad suddenly said, 'Janya, I think you are becoming a bit antisocial. You think too much. And you should get taller. So, I have decided to enroll you in soccer classes.'

I just stared at my father with my mouth open. Okay, first of all, antisocial? Me? Oh, I didn't deserve this.

I would have to go to a sports ground every Monday and Tuesday to practice, he informed me. Soccer, of all games, Dad? Really? What were you thinking? Oh, oh, man. So *this* was what I got for turning a year older.

'Okay,' I said finally, letting out a loud *gulp*. I really wasn't up for an argument at the moment.

'I'm glad you're happy with my decision, Janya,' said Dad. The next time the car stopped, we were home.

Ugh. Why, *why me?* This was sick. Really sick. I think I was *actually sick.* First that weird internal electric shock, and now *this*?

Dad had to go for a meeting later that day. I didn't have any homework to occupy my mind with—not that I felt like studying—so I felt like I was at a loose end. I checked the voicemail messages on our family phone (even if our family only consisted of me, Dad, and our maid, Lalita) because it always provided some kind of entertainment. Lalita had a few days off. Too bad. I liked talking to her.

Dad had mistakenly left one of his phones at home, and as I didn't have anything better to do, I started looking through it (hey, he looks through my stuff too).

Just as I had finished going through his mega-boring notes, emails and reminders (seriously, the man didn't have a single Talking Animals app), I decided to check his messages. And surprise, surprise. Boring messages from seemingly boring people.

But wait…one message caught my attention. It was by this lady called Mandira, and she wrote, 'Hey, it was really nice meeting you today. Oh, and thanks for the job. I look forward to seeing you again tomorrow.' And then there was this weird wink face.

Okay, I guess it was just some random woman that Dad employed in his company. But then the 'what-ifs' began crowding my mind. My inner stalker in fine form, I launched a Facebook search. There were many results, but I narrowed them down because I was pretty sure it couldn't be a 55-year-old white-haired woman with five cats. The Mandira I was looking at seemed uber modern with a slender figure and short, Halle Berry-style hair.

Hmmm, she was probably just a normal human being living a normal life.

I don't know why, but I still wasn't entirely convinced. I decided there was nothing I could do at the moment, except keep my ears peeled.

My Bollywood Moment 4

Back to reality. Tomorrow was Wednesday and I was going to get my results for the tests we had taken before the summer holidays. Everyone knew Aditi and Sanchi would top the class. I guess I would do fine, I mean, I had studied. But I didn't know what was going to happen. Wednesdays were bad. Always bad. They disgusted me from the pit of my stomach.

Sameer was a lucky boy, I thought. He wasn't the one getting his marks. He wasn't the one who would face heartbreak after seeing those horrible numbers. He wasn't the one who knew he would spend the rest of the week sulking.

So I went to school, late as usual, and guess what? I got really good marks—more than 90 per cent in all subjects. How could I, a.k.a. the incompetent shy girl, get better marks than my peers? By peers, of course, I meant Aditi and Sanchi.

Recess was pretty quiet, for some reason. I tried to crack a joke, but both of them gave me a fake laugh and everything went quiet again. I started babbling about my room and how I needed to paint it a new colour.

As I spoke, I realised I felt a bit small around them (mentally, as well as physically. I wasn't the tallest or the strongest or the *smartest* crayon in the pack). It had always been that way, not just today, but now it felt as if waves of iciness were radiating off them. I guess they were just tired or something. I mean, it would be quite exhausting living their all-rounder lives, with sports, studies and boyfriends to manage all together.

They nodded blindly at whatever I said, and didn't quite join in. Soon enough, school got over for the day. The day on which I had gotten high-flying marks in all my subjects. I wanted to shout and let everything out (I could even spout rhymes!)…in a good way. I felt psyched. Everything was awesome at the moment.

I was kind of tired, so after lunch, I lay down on the sofa and decided to listen to the voicemails on our home phone. It was good entertainment, as most of them were weird adverts. I pressed the little speaker button, and as expected, the first one was about some fairness cream. The next one was for Dad from his company—some person had apparently broken their printer. The third one was about popcorn-flavoured bubblegum. Yech. I was getting real tired of this.

And then, the fourth one: 'Hey, Ashish, this is Mandykins! I hope you had a nice day. There were some things I wanted to discuss with you so I was wondering if you would like to have dinner tomorrow, at Les Enchantés? Please call me back as soon as you can. I look forward to hearing from you.' It was like she had the 'wink face' in her voice.

Yes, it wasn't very hard to guess whom this message was from. Mandira, the mystery woman. Wow, I even had a name for her now. Seriously, Janya?

I had to do something, didn't I?

I had to get to the bottom of the 'Mandykins' mystery. *Mandykins, seriously? That's the dumbest nickname she could come up with.* I knew she was upto something. Someone wouldn't just want to go to dinner with Dad *just like that.* And I wasn't being *nosy,* no way. I was just looking out for my father's best interests.

Now, I wasn't really a 'do something' girl. I would rather watch a fight from the sidelines than take someone's side or actually make an effort to stop it. My philosophy was that if the world was continuing to rotate and revolve without my intervention, it meant there was no use for my interference.

But this case…was different. It was about my father. If *he* had heard some guy ask me out to dinner like that, wouldn't he like to do something about it (although circumstances would be different because one, if my father heard someone ask me out, he would go nuts and two, no one in their right mind would ask me out)?

It was Thursday. When I returned from school that afternoon, I went over the plan I had been brainstorming over for two hours, including the silent recess (yes, they were still ignoring me. Were they really tired with their busy lives, or was it something I had done?).

When it was around seven o'clock, Dad told me that he was going out for dinner with work friends. So...he was going out…with *work friends.* Hmmm. Okay, *technically* he was not lying.

Well, so was I. When he left, I called up Lalita. She was going to help me, I had decided. She picked up the phone in a panicky tone after two rings.

'Lalita, this is your boss. It's an emergency. Meet me at the house. And bring the car,' I said, in my best official, manly tone. I felt so confident! (We had gifted Lalita our old used car. She had been working at our place for more than a decade and so we felt she deserved it. Also, no one else would take it.)

After walking around in circles for what seemed like a millennium, the doorbell finally rang.

'What happened?' Lalita asked even before she entered the house. 'I thought your father had called me!'

Wow, I really sounded like Dad?

'You have to take me somewhere,' I told her. 'I'll explain it to you on the way.' After a lot of foggy explanations and frantic queries for directions to the restaurant, we finally found the place. It was quite fancy. Fancy enough for people to throw suspicious glances at us because of the banged-up old car Lalita and I pulled up in.

'You really think this is smart?' she asked me.

'I don't know. Let's just pray it works out.'

It was time to get into action. I had worn a black dress to make me look grown-up and sophisticated. *EEP*! I was *so* scared. A rush of nervousness passed through me when I saw a waiter coming my way.

'Table for two?' he asked me, in a forced British accent which I found totally annoying. It sounded like he was being strangled.

'Yeah,' I said.

He led me to a beautifully decorated table, with weird mushy stuff on it (by mushy, I mean roses and candles and all that. What was the deal with candles on a dinner table?

If I owned a restaurant, I would never allow it. Not unless I wanted it to burn down).

'May I get you the menu?' he asked me in that same 'refined' tone.

'No, I'll wait for some time,' I said.

'Sure, mademoiselle.'

Did I really look like a 25-year-old? Wait, is that a good thing? I mean, I *was* wearing my highest heels (which were only two inches, though) and I was pretty clumsy in them. I was hoping I wouldn't fall. That was one of the infinite ways my plan could backfire. God…I really didn't want to think about the consequences if *that* happened. *Shudder.*

I searched the restaurant for a dark-haired man wearing a dark blue shirt. I couldn't find anyone who resembled that description. What if I had come to the wrong restaurant? I decided to wait and see for some time. But I hated waiting. It drove me nuts. This was pure agony.

Then I saw him. Dad. It was like blood rushed into my veins again. I was not in the wrong place! Yes! I hoped he wouldn't recognise me. But I knew he would not, for he had lived with me long enough to know I didn't wear dresses.

Soon enough, the lady reached too. I guess I had looked at the right Facebook page, she was every bit of her profile picture, with tanned skin and a lean, size zero figure. I don't know why, but I was reminded of Maya at that moment. Both of them looked fake. And perfect.

The main purpose of the plan was to hear what they were talking about, and see if the lady was right for him. And, of course, to check out how 'Mandykins' looked and behaved. I looked around. Which table? My intuition told me to hide below one in the corner, over there, the one I found the prettiest. I pretended to drop my purse (I couldn't believe I was carrying a purse. I hated purses. What the hell was one supposed to carry in them? I mean, I had seen many girls my age with purses. What did they carry in them? Make-up? Pocket money? Guns? I was against make-up and I did not get pocket money. I would love to carry guns in my purse, though. What a handy way of killing people!).

Anyway, that useless accessory gave me a good excuse for being on the ground. I slithered my way out from below that table to another. I ducked under it and found myself sitting in the middle of two adults. I was praying it was the table I wanted, when I heard a really familiar voice. It was Dad alright. The other voice I heard was a screechy toad's, capable of shattering glass for miles. They were looking at the food that was on the menu.

Dad asked, 'So, Mandira, do you prefer the Caesar salad with the mayonnaise or without?'

'Without, please. I'm on a strict diet,' the toad screeched.

'May I take your order, sir?' the annoying waiter asked.

'Um...I would like a Coke. What about you?' That's Dad ordering my favourite drink.

'Sparkling water.'

Seriously? I did *not* like this lady. *Sparkling water*! Ewww.

Dad was furiously shaking his leg. He did that a lot when he was nervous. Mandira, meanwhile, stayed still in her four-inch stilettos.

'So what did you do earlier, before you came to my company?'

'Hmm…nothing special, just small odd jobs.' Mandira said with hesitation in her voice.

'Like what?' Dad asked, visibly curious.

Silence. I thought that they had discovered me. I felt as if I had frozen. *Oh no,* I thought. *How in the world could I possibly explain this situation to my father?*

'Well, I used to be a teacher. In kindergarten.'

BZZT!!! Whoa. I was on the edge of blowing my cover, but luck saved me. That terrible twinge inside me again? I hadnt felt it for *days.*

'Really? Oh that's wonderful. You must be *great* with children.' Dad sounded pleased.

'Well, yeah. Children just stick to me like bees to honey.'

BZZT!!! Again? *Really?* What was going on? I already had enough on my mind, and I was hoping that the shocks were just a one-time thing. But *no.* They had to come back to haunt me. And at this very precarious moment.

'That's wonderful.'

'You know,' she said, 'I'm pretty sure you must be a great boss.'

Okay. *Now* she was just trying to flatter Dad. Well, she couldn't be better than me. I had perfected the art of wrapping him around my little finger. I didn't want anyone else to have the same privilege.

'Um, that's very nice of you to think so.' Dad's voice was now a bit distant.

'So, uh, how was work?' Dad asked.

'Nice, I guess. But I think you need a new general manager. Your company is growing fast,' Mandira screeched.

'Oh, really? Who do you suggest?'

'Someone like me,' she screeched a bit more.

'But I like Kunika. She is doing a pretty fine job,' Dad said, trying to defend his current GM.

Kunika was so cool. She would always bring me candy when I was small. Wait, she still did. And Dad would be like, awww, man, don't spoil her. But she was awesome. I felt so mad. How dare she say that? You go, Dad!

'Have you seen the clothes she wears? All grey. I mean, she's so boring,' continued Mandira.

After battling for a few minutes against her senseless reasons—all in vain—Dad said, 'Hmmm, I don't know. I'll think about it. It's just that she's been with us for almost 11 years now, and it would be unfair to demote her. But you have a point. We need something new.'

She *was* trying to manipulate him! Did she think she was the queen of the world? My ears were burning. But why did she want to be the general manager? It wasn't *such* a good position.

I sat there till they finished. After eating what seemed like their main course, Dad said, 'Oh, look at the time, it's almost 11. I can't leave Janya alone for such a long time. She'll start to worry.'

Awww! Dad cared about me! Well, duh.

'Who's this Janya?' Mandira asked. How *dare* she call me *this* Janya? I felt like taking a knife and cutting off her long, lean, skinny legs, which was all I could see of her.

'She's my daughter. She's the most perfect girl in the world. She's good at everything...studies, sports...'

'But what about me?'

'I'm so sorry. I forgot to order dessert,' Dad said.

Dessert? Haha. Good one, Dad. I could see that he was trying to change the subject, like I had to do with Maya. But this woman was too persistent, or maybe too thick, to get the hint.

'No, I mean, don't you think she's a little too small to be perfect? Aren't *I* perfect?' demanded Mandira.

'Oh, yeah. You are too,' Dad said, feeling a bit embarrassed. What else could he say when faced with a banshee like her? I had a feeling Mandira wasn't going to like me all that much; if she ever met me, that is.

They got up and walked away, and I was left crouching under the table.

I hadn't thought about this part. How was I going to get out without anybody noticing? The table was kind of in the middle of the room. What was I supposed to do? Suddenly, a cart stopped close by to clear the table. I got into the empty shelf underneath on which they keep dishes and glasses and stuff. It was draped all round with a purple velvet cloth and, luckily, I was a perfect fit...small enough to get inside. When no one was looking, I climbed out, and while rushing away, I bumped into the waiter with the strangulated accent.

Uh oh. The food he was carrying fell down and he bumped into a table. There were candles on it, which fell and set it on fire. Duh. They should have followed my rules for a candle-less existence.

My plan seemed to have gone haywire, right at the very end.

I ran for my life, squeezing past customers and hotel staff. I got spaghetti on my head. I had to dodge other platters of food and drink. Those who were eating stood up and stared with their mouths open. This was a wild-goose chase—the strangle-voiced waiter chasing a spaghetti-haired girl who had set a restaurant on fire. I lost him quite soon; he was too fat to run as fast as me.

When I was outside, I tried to find Lalita, but she wasn't anywhere to be seen. What if I couldn't locate her in time? Dad would already have reached home by now! He would find out everything I had done! My life was so over. But I couldn't lose hope, could I? I had to do something! I couldn't let the story finish like this! I combed through the parking lot, didn't find her anywhere. I was really, really worried now. What if Dad reached home and didn't find me there, and I came back hours later draped in spaghetti? He would think I had some kind of weird double life which involved a fetish for spaghetti.

I found Lalita in the underground parking lot. I had never been happier to sit inside a car. But the joy dissipated somewhat when she began driving like a madwoman. I was in the passenger seat praying for my life. None of us wanted to get into trouble.

Luckily, I was home in minutes, and I thanked my stars that Dad hadn't reached yet. I hastily took a shower. I also made Lalita swear on her life that she would not utter a word of this to anyone. I trusted her.

When Dad came back, I tried to act as if nothing had happened. I began questioning him, 'Dad, what's up? Why did you come home so late?'

He replied, 'Oh, nothing. There was just so much traffic.

BZZT!!!

My stomach began to lurch and my knees were shaking badly. I felt that *shock* again, the same one I had felt when Sanchi was going on and on about how crazy her 'boyfriend' was about her, and the same one I had felt just an hour ago. Wow, I couldn't believe it had just been an hour since I got out of that hellhole.

I didn't say anything. There had to be a reason he wasn't telling me that he had been on a *date* with Mandira. Ugh, 'date' sounded so weird.

My head started aching really badly after the 'shock' and I didn't feel good. I didn't even want to think about the 'shock' or the 'date' or anything.

I just wanted to sleep.

Bad Timing, Everywhere 5

The whole weekend went by very slowly. I felt like I was crawling through it. On Monday, I woke up late, and Dad was still sleeping. It was 7:10 a.m. The first bell in school would ring in 15 minutes. I had only five minutes to dress up and chug my milk (I didn't have breakfast in the morning, I never felt like eating that early). I hurriedly put on my stupid school uniform—a buttoned-up shirt (like in every other Indian school) and a skirt. Our school had the un-trendiest clothes possible in the whole world. When I woke Dad up, he shot out of bed like a bullet and made me a *parantha* in record time. The 'Self-Service Restaurant' was always closed on Mondays. (Lalita was still on leave, but she had earned it, I guess. I owed her.)

With only five minutes to go before my first class, Dad dropped me to school. The stupid guard was just closing the gate and, quick as a flash, he let Rahul get in, but not me. Rahul was in the other section and I hated him (by that, I mean I *intensely* disliked him) because his mother was a teacher at the school and so he got partial treatment. He thoroughly enjoyed, and abused, that privilege.

Anyway, the dumb guard refused to open the gate for me. I had to get my name written in the 'late' register from the other gate.

A school prefect was standing there, talking to someone on her swanky touch screen phone. I told her my name and which class I was in, but she was too busy talking to her boyfriend to even notice me. *Ugh.* Older people and their boyfriends. It made me sick.

'Um, hello?' I said at last, at the top of my annoyed voice.

'What?' she noticed me and sneered.

'I'm late.'

'Whatever,' she said, and returned to her 'deep' conversation after she wrote my name and class number. I let out a sigh and hurried to my classroom.

The first bell rang as I was negotiating my way through a mob of 10th graders fighting (I didn't get it. Why did older people keep fighting all the time? To gain attention? That was just weak. But it was good entertainment for the spectators). It indicated the time for class and it also meant that I was freaking late. I was running quite weirdly—half-running, half-jogging—to my class. Just as I arrived at the door and stepped in, almost panting, I realised everyone was smiling at me.

Was there spinach stuck in my teeth (that didn't even make sense. I didn't eat breakfast). Was toilet paper stuck to my shoe? Why was everyone grinning like that?

I later discovered the answer. Mrs. Miglani, was taking attendance and I had arrived just at the moment when it was my turn to say 'Present, ma'am'. Okay, yes, it was a coincidence. But why did everyone have to crack up like that? Were their lives so lacking in humour that they had to laugh at every pathetic thing they saw? How sad. The saddest part was that I was one of them.

In Geography, our teacher had a 'surprise' for us. (God, I had started dreading that word.)

'Good morning ma'am,' we chorused in the dull sing-song tone nearly all students around the world use in every school (our Geography teacher was male, but we were so used to saying 'ma'am' that we didn't care. Neither did most of the teachers).

'Yeah, yeah,' Mr. Raj mumbled. 'Today I have a surprise for you.'

'Yay,' said the whole class (not cheered, *said*).

'Yesh, I ekshpekted you to be happy. For our first semester project thish year, you will work with your ashigned partners. I will tell you shumthing about it now.'

'Boo.' Everyone began mumbling.

'Quiet!' he hissed, and then told us 'shumthing' about the project. I knew what working with a partner meant. It usually meant I would do all of the work because the other person would either be too lazy or just not care...and we would both get equal credit. Well, that was life.

But this time, things would (hopefully) be different.

I would be working with my 'ashingned' partner, 'Shameer'! Ahem. We had a LOT of research to do as we were supposed to write a 1,000-word essay on global warming.

Mr. Raj also said that we could use the school computers. Our work had to be submitted in two weeks, or else (he didn't say anything after that, I think he expected us to be scared or something).

While he was talking, Mandira's exasperating face was still spinning in my head. I could still feel the evil thoughts that had radiated out of her when I was under the table That Day. I didn't exactly know what she wanted, but I knew that she wasn't good. Even back then,

I had felt those unexplainable electrical shocks in my stomach every time she tried to convince Dad she was telling him the right thing to do. I think I had developed an internal circuit which was slowly making me weaker day by day. Perhaps I was going to collapse one day without warning.

'So when do you want to start working on the project?' I asked Sameer casually, trying not to sound too eager. I didn't want to sound extra keen, you know. I just wanted to act *cool.*

'Uh...I don't know. When do you want to start?' Sameer replied. Oh, the way he spoke. Such a manly voice (it made all the other boys in our class look like five-year-olds). I did my best to resist such thoughts and pulled myself back into the present.

'Well. We'll start tomorrow, I guess. Why don't you book a computer, otherwise we won't get one,' I suggested.

'Okay, I'll do that during recess.'

I waited. I waited. And I kept on waiting, till he finally said, 'Where...um...HOW do we book a computer?'

'I knew you were going to ask me that,' I said, with a sly smile. 'I'll show you. Do you mind? I mean, do you mind skipping a bit of recess?'

'Uh...not at all,' he said in a weird tone.

YAY!!! I was going to take Sameer to the Computer Lab in the break! Only one period from now!

Again, time slowed down so much I practically felt it stand still. But finally, there it was. The recess bell.

While I was trying to locate my tiffin box in my bag, I realised I was making Sameer wait for me. I shouldn't do that. 'Meet me at The Chat,' I told him, in a hurried tone, and we temporarily parted.

The Chat is the place where all students of the 10th, 11th and 12th grades were seen chatting in their free periods. Some Head Boy or someone had named it (unofficially) The Chat. But I thought that name was totally lacking in creativity. Wasn't it a stupid name? The Chat.

But who was I to judge? Just a mere eighth grader. I made it to The Chat after I got out from the deserted school building (no one except prefects and teachers were allowed to stay inside, and if you did, there was no knowing what would happen. Maybe the prefects were being hypnotised by the teachers' evil forces and working on something even more stupendously boring than school). It was crowded with students from the higher grades. I even noticed the girl I had interrupted from her precious phone call that morning. Thank goodness she wasn't still stuck to her phone or my eye-roll would've been off the charts.

Aditi and Sanchi were still ignoring me so I didn't really bother talking to them.

Sameer was nowhere in sight. Where *was* he? After nearly 20 seconds trying to figure that out, it hit me. He probably didn't know what The Chat was! Or where.

Oooooh! There he was! I spotted him. He had this confused look on his face which made him look so *adorable*! Oh man. There was no going back as far as this not-falling-for-Sameer attempt was concerned. The water was now *way* over my head.

'Hey! Sameer! I'm here!' I called out to him, but not so loudly that all the other students would stare at me.

'Oh, uh...I'm sorry. I didn'*t know w*here it was...the... uh, what was it *ag*ain?' he asked.

'The Chat,' I said, trying not to ogle at him in a way that was too obvious.

'I get it,' he smiled. He could have sold it for a million rupees. His smile, I mean.

'Um, okay,' I said, my cheeks burning. What if he hated girls who kept blushing all the time?

Just then, the darn bell rang and brought our lovely conversation to an end. Sometimes I wondered if the school bell was possessed by the devil. It always wanted to put an end to good things. Okay, maybe not always—I had to thank it for ringing when our never-ending Science period was going on.

'Damn,' Sameer mumbled. My thoughts exactly.

'Well, we'll do it tomorrow, then,' I said, a hint of regret in my voice.

'Tomorrow,' he repeated, and walked away.

Goodbye, Sanity 6

School after that was...good. It was actually good. I enjoyed it. That didn't happen often. I generally disliked that part of my routine existence. I wasn't saying that because I was bitter or anything. But it wasn't like school was video game heaven.

'Hey, Janya. How was your day?' Dad asked me like he did everyday at the same time as I climbed into the car after school was over. 'Awesome,' I smiled at him. This time, it wasn't a fake smile. After I went home, I felt so much at peace that I decided to take a crack at my homework and finish it off so I could spend the rest of the day lounging around the house.

Dad came back early from office that day.

'Dad, don't you have a meeting or something today?'

'Don't you have to go for your soccer classes?' he asked in reply. Oh, my god. I can't believe I forgot. *So that's* why I was feeling so happy. I knew something was wrong. Dad would be in the gym—the air-conditioned gym—and I would be stuck in the scorching heat on a football ground.

I knew it. Things were going too 'vell' (that's how Mr. Raj says it) to last for too long.

I reached the place by 10 minutes past six. Dad delayed us by talking on the phone. The driver was home, sick, so he had to drive the car himself. On the way, some *friend* of his called. He pulled over to the side (claiming he had to talk because it was 'awfully urgent'). I was left all alone in the car. It must have been Mandira on the line. I was trying to overhear their conversation but it was too hard, considering he was outside. I turned on the radio. The first thing I heard was a corny love song from a movie. That bugged me a lot.

When I couldn't take it anymore, I scolded Dad and told him to get in the car, otherwise I would not play football. He got in after a minute and began to drive. Sometimes I really thought Dad just forgot about everything. Including me.

Wait.

I was *not* going to think about Mom. I was *not* going to think about Mom. I was *not* going to think about Mom. I didn't want to cry. But I couldn't stop thinking about her. I didn't even get to celebrate Mother's Day. Not fair. After 10 minutes we finally reached that sports place. I was glad, in a way. I wanted to be distracted from thoughts of my mother.

'Okay, well, I'll drop you to the field and then go to the gym.'

Dad picked up my water bottle for me. I looked around. It was the same building I had been to That Day (spaghetti hair...rings a bell?). Oh, memories.

In front of me stood a shiny structure with a bubbling fountain on either side. And a glass door manned by two WWE wrestler-type guards. Great.

But really, I thought, as I walked the path to the field in what seemed like 6x slow motion, what other choice did I have? I couldn't go back to the car. I didn't even have the keys. And everyone would think I was a freak. Sometimes I thought I really was one.

When we reached the field, there was a plump, strict-looking teacher (I had been a student for enough years to know after just one look whether a teacher was strict or not) standing there, with a whistle around his neck.

'New? Janya?' he asked me. I was wearing a T-shirt with a one-liner—a cheeky insult—on it (I owned plenty of such shirts; what could I say, I just didn't like people and wanted to discourage them from talking to me) and a pair of shorts. It was really warm that day.

'Uh...yeah,' I stammered.

'Well, you are an hour late. You are in the beginners' class, and it was moved up an hour so it's over now,' the coach said in a very uptight tone.

'Oh.'

Damn! Couldn't the damn teacher have told me before? What a douchenozzle!

'Do you want to play today? You can join the seniors.'

I could have said no.

'Uh...okay.'

I wanted to slap myself for saying the opposite of what I was thinking, but if I had refused, the coach would think of me as a scared little wimp.

The rest of the hour was hell. I don't know how I got through it, but I did. First of all, all the kids in the class were much older than me and massively built. They were so tall and scary, how could I be expected to keep up with them? Okay, okay. I guess I was overreacting. They looked my age. But still. I had a feeling I wasn't going to like them. They weren't even talking to me. I wish I had said no to joining in, and then gone with Dad to walk on the treadmill.

After half the class had somehow gone by, we were told to play a match. A few minutes in, I started hyperventilating. Oh man. What now? Should I ask if I could sit down? Or would everyone think I was a freak? Or maybe I should keep running? What the heck.

'Sir, can I sit down? I am feeling dizzy,' I said, huffing and puffing, barely able to catch my breath.

'Go,' he muttered, and went back to tell the others they were walking incorrectly or something. I sat down on the sort-of-wet grass, constantly looking at my watch and worrying about whether I would be made to play some more.

Ugh. I wished I was invisible. What would these other girls be thinking now? Probably something bad about me.

After what seemed like an era, the class ended and I prepared to make my way to the gym. I could hear the others laughing. What kind of people were they? How could they enjoy such a boring (and scary) class? I was sure the Beginners' Group would be way better than this.

I was heading back to the main building when a girl—she seemed to be in 9th grade—started talking to me, 'Today was nice, right?' She asked me. Small talk. *Excellent*. Just what I wanted.

'Yeah, it was fun.'

'You know, I've been playing here for almost a year now. And I have to admit, I'm just too good.'

Was she trying to make me feel bad? I knew how much I sucked.

'You know, I used to be in my school's football team.'

'You *used* to?' I asked, even though I didn't really give a crap.

'Yeah. I quit because I was better than all the other players. It was just too easy to outplay them.'

BZZT!!!! Ugh, the vibration again! I felt all tingly. My head felt light.

'No. You didn't quit.' I couldn't stop the words as they tumbled off my tongue.

'What do you mean?'

'They...they kicked you out. They kicked you out and demoted you to an alternative's role because you were too bossy and uncooperative.'

What? What did I just say? No, I did not say that.

Silence.

'No...no, they didn't! You don't even have any right to say that, weirdo!' She started sweating profusely and breathing heavily, eventually hurrying away.

I did *not* say that. I don't even know anything about that girl. I saw her today for the first time. She wasn't incorrect; I had no right to say all that. But the words *did* come out of my mouth. I was the only one standing and talking to her. There was no one else around me. What if everything I said was true? What if she *was* kicked out? Oh, I didn't care about the damn girl! I just wanted to know the reason for the damn vibrations and why my tongue had taken on a life of its own. I stuck it out and tried examining it… crossing my eyes in the process. But it looked completely human. What if I said all that because I was jealous after all her boasting, and I made something up just to embarrass her? But I would never do that. I didn't like being mean, especially to people I didn't even *know*. I was hearing myself say those words, but I couldn't stop myself. It was like someone else had possessed me for that fraction of time. The words just started pouring out of my mouth, and I couldn't put a lid on it.

I felt deranged. I felt betrayed by my own mouth. This was definitely connected to the random electric shocks I had felt *multiple* times now. I had to stop kidding myself. No way was it a one-time thing. My brain felt numb. I had a huge headache, like the one on the Day of the Spaghetti.

What the *hell* was wrong with me?

The Crush Cycle 7

When I found the gym at last, I pleaded with Dad to take me home. I just wanted to collapse, even if it was on the hot concrete floor. I felt exhausted and confused.

The next morning, I woke up by myself. I shook Dad awake (like I regularly did these days, as if I didn't have enough responsibilities) and he sleepily dropped me to school. Late, again, but this time the stupid guard let me in.

'Janya!' Someone called out to me.

I looked back, hoping it would be Sameer. I hoped with all my might. But, as I was the unluckiest girl in the world, it was...Maya.

'Uh. Hi,' I said, disappointed.

'So! What's up with you?' Maya's tone had a few thousand rainbows thrown in. Ugh. Sickeningly sweet.

'I...uh...'

There was a *lot* of stuff up with me but Maya was, literally, the last person in this world I could pour my heart out to. What would have happened if the earth had actually exploded on December 21, 2012, and everyone was dead except Maya and me? That was the worst situation I could imagine.

'Where were you during recess yesterday? We had Burger Special.'

Thank *goodness* I missed that. I would have had to gulp down a tasteless burger and then would definitely have thrown up. After that, of course, everybody would think of me as a freak. Like my teammates had at soccer.

'Uh...I had to go to...the dentist during recess...,' I stammered. 'It was an emergency, my tooth had starting aching all of a sudden and I felt really sick.'

Was that all I could come up with? Seriously?

'Oh. My father's uncle's friend's brother is a dentist, and he works in this really famous hospital in the US. It is one of the best hospitals in the world, you know.'

Why did she have to brag about everything? First, where she went on her vacation, and now *about a dentist*?! If there was a category like Best Boaster in a book of world records, I am sure Maya would win it hands down. I mean, she could even boast about dentists. What more do you need in a top-class boaster?

It turned out that there was no assembly that day, due to a sudden downpour. The announcement saved me from more ridiculous boasts from the Best Boaster in the World. Not much later, though, the rain stopped and the weather became even worse. The sun shone really bright and then everything was moist and sticky. I really, really hated it.

We were supposed to go to the computer lab that day, but Sameer had to finish his History homework—like half the other class members—so we had to wait till recess again.

'Okay, come on. You aren't going to get lost today,' I said, leading Sameer to the crowded fire exit (which had never been used for its intended purpose because there had never been a fire in our school. Except that one time... never mind, that's a long story).

'How are we going to make it through this?' Sameer asked me.

'Okay. Stay close, otherwise you could really get hurt.'

'Me? Hurt?' he chuckled.

'We're going in.' I felt like superheroes did right before they took on a scary assignment. The crush of students represented the enemies I had to kill. I dove into the madding crowd and we powered through till we emerged on the other side.

'Whoa! I could have been seriously dead! I owe my life to you,' said Sameer, squinting in the bright, bright sun.

'Ha, ha. Real funny.'

'No, really. I'm serious. I owe you eternal servitude. I could have been run over in that stampede and then the world would have changed. They would probably have put a ban on staircases and we would have to use elevators, or ramps. Even those would get overloaded and then the elevators would come crashing down to the ground. Then they would put a ban on elevators.

'So, only the ramps would be left. Someone would fall off their low railings, and those would be banned too. Ultimately, the school wouldn't be able to function because there would be no way to move between floors,' Sameer said all this in one breath.

Wow. He was so damn creative! He wasn't just all about the looks (well, I did judge a person only by his looks because I was shallow, but Sameer was just as good on the inside). He was quiet and timid for so long but in a flash, he had conjured up such imaginative scenarios in his head, jumping from one thought to another. And that too, on my favourite topic—the end of school. What a brain! I could see The Cycle beginning.

The Crush Cycle:

Stage One: You see him for the first time and feel your heart skip a beat. You can't wait to see him again. You think, oh my god, he is my Adonis.

Stage Two: You try to impress him in every way possible to get his attention. You feel really impatient all the time if you don't see him, like something wants to burst open from your insides. You feel really fidgety and want to see that person *all the freaking time*. Basically, you go nuts.

Stage Three: You become good friends and talk a lot. Or, if not, like in my case, you just smile at each other while getting a severe urge to strike up a conversation. It seems like the reason you are living is to see him. You may even get dreams about him. This is the peak of the Cycle.

Stage Four: Your 'relationship' starts falling apart a bit and you don't get the giddy feeling of Stage One. You feel slightly empty and start realising all the stupid things you did for that Special Someone and curse yourself repeatedly.

Stage Five: You feel he is nothing special anymore and don't feel that spark when you see him again. You might think, 'Oh, isn't it that guy?' in your head. Much later, you remember him again, but only to recall the Good Old Days.

The Cycle may repeat itself in rare cases. *Very* rare cases. So that was the Crush Cycle. Please don't tell anyone about it. It's definitely the girliest thing I had ever thought of.

'Wow.' That was my only response after his brain had blown me away.

'Uh, let's go to the computer lab before the stupid bell rings again and spoils everything,' he said as I led him to the Activity Building, through The Chat. All the seniors reeked of perfumes (girls) and deodorants (boys), which made it a welter of weird smells. As we entered the block, which was in a senior section building, a group of 12th grade boys started walking in our direction. They were so stinky that my eyes began watering as they passed. 'Ugh!' I coughed in disgust.

We were hurrying up the narrow boys' stairs. Now, I didn't know why there were different sets of stairs for boys and girls, but the boys' stairs were narrower and you could easily slip on them, while the girls' stairs were safer and broad. But the former were a shortcut to the Computer Lab, and we were really in a hurry.

'I...feel like...I've made it to...Mount Everest!' said an out-of-breath Sameer when we reached the Lab on the fourth floor, *by the stairs,* a.k.a. the route to Mount Everest.

'Shut up,' I said, jokingly. But it wasn't a bad comparison. The only difference was that it wasn't cold. (It did get freezing in the winter, though). God, I couldn't believe I was appreciating his dumb one-liners. I was well and truly entrenched in The Cycle.

We took off our shoes in front of the lab like two law-abiding students (The *teachers* wore their shoes inside the lab, but we weren't allowed to. It was quite silly. We only wore our school shoes to school...but the teachers had no such uniform; they wore them at other places too. The rule should have been the other way around).

The teacher, Mrs. Agarwal, gestured to us to come in and greeted us very cheerfully. She was one of my favourite teachers.

'Ma'am, we have this Geography project...'

'I have the entire 8th grade coming to me and I know about your project. But I'm really sorry, all the computers are already taken,' she said, while searching for something on her desk. 'You should go to the library in the basement. Here's a permission slip. It's good if you go there; the printers work really well.'

The piece of paper had her signature and something else written in super cursive handwriting that only professional readers would be able to understand, if there was such a thing as professional readers.

'Thank you so much, ma'am,' I said, and then we climbed down the steep stairs.

'Oh, man. If the library teachers say "No", we are doomed,' moaned Sameer.

'I'm sure they'll allow us to work.' I was trying to keep a 'positive attitude'; it was one of those times when I could do that and not think of the worst case scenario. Otherwise, every uncomfortable situation made me mostly want to say, 'I'm scared. I'm scared. I'm going to die!' Paranoid much?

We had reached.

'Good morning, sir,' I said.

'Good morning. What do you want, both of you?' Mr. Tiwari replied in a crabby tone.

'Um, here is a note from Mrs. Agarwal...,' I said, handing him the permission slip. He looked at it and pointed to a machine.

'Well, we got ourselves a computer. I didn't think it would happen,' said Sameer as he bent down to turn on the UPS.

'Thank goodness...,' I sighed, when the age-old *dabba* of a computer came on. I didn't think *that* would happen. Why did they even *keep* such old Windows 98 computers in the school? Hadn't they heard of an LCD, or, dare I say, LED? Windows 8, anyone?

'This thing is really slow,' Sameer complained.

'Yeah. Even Macs are better than this piece of junk.'

'Hey, have you checked out that new slim Mac?'

We yapped like this while waiting for the computer to boot. I was glad I got the chance to show him I was totally clued in on the latest technology, and didn't spend my days worrying about the right shade of lip gloss or the perfect dress—the concerns of *every* girl my age.

'Yeah. But they aren't very good because most video games don't work on them. You can't even download anything without those stupid permissions. My friend has one and she keeps wanting to break it, but she can't because it costs around a thousand trillion rupees.'

Sameer chuckled. 'True.'

'Okay, the computer is on. Let's start doing our research,' I said, even though my mind was the farthest from a boring Geography project as it could be. I was sitting with the best person in the world (kind of), I shouldn't have to work! He felt like the best person right now, anyway. Aditi and Sanchi had been acting very weird. I had to sit with Smitha (the quiet girl) in Math again because neither of them looked my way even once.

During the Good Old Days, Aditi and I used to sit together, and Sanchi used to sit with the other girl, Smitha. Whatever. I had more important things to handle. I was sitting next to a *Greek god*!

And we had work to do.

We were concentrating completely on figuring out the introduction to our project, when I noticed that the whole library was *deserted*.

Pimply Situations 8

'Oh, CRAP.' I hoped it wasn't true. But it was. *We didn't hear the bell ring.*

'What?' asked Sameer.

'Look around.'

'We're late, aren't we?' he asked in an uneasy tone.

'Nope. We're not just late. We're *toast.* Shut off the computer from the main switch. It doesn't matter if it never works again. If we're late for English, you *do not* want to face Mrs. Goel.'

He followed my instructions because we both knew what had happened to Alisha when she got late. You don't want to know.

I felt so pimply (that's what I called the feeling when something really humiliating happened because of me. The incident was like a pimple. You managed to get rid of it somehow, but it always left a scar. *Shudder*).

Turning off the computer from the UPS was regarded as a major criminal offence in our school, but the only person there was Mr. Tiwari, daydreaming. We got away with our crime.

We still had a chance to make it to class in the nick of time. We dashed out of the library. Oh, no. Those smelly 12th-ees were coming this way.

'Watch out!' yelled Sameer. I didn't notice when the steps began. Oh yeah. I tumbled down a full flight of stairs in front of the whole wide world. There were only four steps that I missed. But still, *ow.*

'Oof,' I managed to utter when I was flat on my face. The world seemed so different from down here. All you could see was concrete and stones. And ants. Ants scared me. They have those creepy little feelers...UGH! I could see particles of gravel on the cement ground. They were in countless shades of grey. I didn't even know that grey came in so many varieties. I could feel the vibration of basketballs as they hit the ground. I could hear rapid footsteps coming nearer...

'Oh, my god. Here, let me help you.' I heard Sameer's voice. 'Janya, your knee is bleeding. Really badly.'

I looked down to see that my right knee had a lot of blood around it, like a pond of blood, right there on my knee. It was funny how I didn't even feel the pain. I guess I was too busy 'blushing' while thinking about how caring Sameer was.

'Oh. I didn't feel it,' I said, feeling awkward. Well, I couldn't say 'OW!' again, or he would think I was one of those girly-girls who cried even when they got a little bruise. *Oh my god, look at me, I broke my nail. Boo-hoo!*

'Come on. Let's go to the doctor.'

'No, really, I'm fine.'

'No, really, you're not. Forget it. I am taking you to the doctor's room, and that is final.'

I shrugged. I mean, it *was* paining, once Sameer told me about it, anyway. If he hadn't, maybe I wouldn't have to waste my time going to the doctor. Well, if he hadn't said anything, I would have been walking around with a huge scrape on my knee. My friends—as if I *had* any—would have been disgusted at the sight.

Sameer practically dragged me to the infirmary, which took five minutes despite being close by. I was so touched that he had stayed by my side. I guess there *were* people in the world who cared about others...or maybe he didn't go because now he had an excuse to tell Mrs. Goel for coming late. Sigh, the ugly truth.

I told the doctor that I had fallen down the stairs but she was so mean, she didn't even console me while I was howling in pain. The medicine stung. A *lot.*

I was sure Sameer wanted to get away now. But he just stood there, waiting for me so we could go to class. The mean doctor said it would be better if I left the wound uncovered while the medicine dried (okay, *EW!)* and then she would put a crepe bandage if I wanted. Oh yeah, I wanted one because anyone who saw the freshly formed scab would throw up. I didn't want to be the reason people threw up.

'Well, half the period is already over,' Sameer informed me.

I felt *so* messed up. 'I don't want to go back to class,' I grumbled as we made our way through an empty basketball court.

'Neither do I,' Sameer replied, nodding his head. 'It'll be so weird entering the class.'

'Can I just sit down for a while? My leg is stinging like hell.'

'Sure.'

We made our way to this place I really liked. There was a lemon tree in the school ground which provided great shade, and if you sat underneath it, no one could see you because it leaned like the Tower of Pisa. Our English teacher sure couldn't spot us. She had the knack of showing up when students weren't in their scheduled classes.

'Wow. This is such a nice place.'

'We're not bunking, are we?' I asked. I wanted to scream, I wanted to shout. There were words inside me that couldn't wait to come out (*I was rhyming again*! I think it happened when I was nervous).

Sameer smirked and snorted. 'NO!'

I raised an eyebrow.

'Well,' he looked down. 'Kinda...'

'Feels exciting,' I said. I didn't want to stay silent for long. I couldn't just sit there like a shy little girly-girl.

'Yeah,' he said, waiting for me to continue the dead conversation.

'This is so cool. Have you ever bunked?' I asked him, still getting the urge to scream.

'Not really. Have you?' he asked, looking at me with those dark Bourneville eyes. If I could just eat them up....

'Nah. I'm a good girl, you know,' I laughed, and so did he. I didn't want English period to end. Everything was quiet for a while, but it seemed like eternity. I wanted to pause everything around me and let out the loudest scream, I was filled with so much adrenaline. I glanced at Sameer. He was sweating, for some reason. He seemed to be thinking of something very deeply. If only I could read minds.

'Uh...Janya...,' he stammered. 'I wanted to tell you something.'

'What?' I asked, thinking of the possibilities. What was he going to say?

'Well, I think I kind of...'

CLANG! There went the *freaking* bell, putting an end to both our fantasies, especially mine.

'Well, we better get going. We don't want the teacher to spot us.' Sameer got up, looking slightly frazzled.

But what was he going to say back then? Aargh! That devil-possessed bell!

I grunted. I didn't feel like speaking. We made our way to the classroom through crowded corridors—pushing past girls going to the washroom while boys stared at them. Sameer and I got separated for a while. It felt weird, know what I mean?

There was always havoc in the school after the bell rang. It was almost like a chaotic volcano erupting on a calm, peaceful island. We quietly entered the class and, to our relief, no one paid us any attention. There was obviously no teacher in the classroom because of the eardrum-shattering level of sound.

~

It was time for Punjabi class. Now, you would think I was REALLY strange to have chosen Punjabi. But I wanted to do something different from my *other* friends (basically Aditi) who had been stuck in Sanskrit class every zero period. I liked Punjabi. It was better than Sanskrit. When I grew up and started working, I definitely wouldn't need Sanskrit. But I may need Punjabi a *lot*. Well, maybe I would need French too, but whatever. I didn't think I was going to be a fashion designer (or whatever else you associate with France).

Five minutes later, the Punjabi teacher finally entered. Everyone, including Sameer, was sitting with their friends and I was sitting alone. Aditi was in Sanskrit, but Sanchi had taken Punjabi too. We normally sat together but, as it had been happening recently, she was sitting with Smitha today. I didn't want to think about them. I had enough on my mind anyway.

But then I remembered that I had lent my notebook to Sanchi, and she was supposed to return it a week ago. I went up to her.

'Which notebook?' she asked, trying to act completely innocent.

'My Punjabi notebook. You had borrowed it from me two weeks ago, and were supposed to return it last week.'

'What are you talking about? I didn't borrow any Punjabi notebook!' she exclaimed.

BZZT!!!

The jolt went through my whole body and words started spilling out of my mouth uncontrollably.

'Yes, you did. You have it in your bag right now. You were going to dump it before class started, but the teacher called you for some work so you decided to shred it in the staff room in the next period. You were going to behave like nothing ever happened.'

What the…?

What was I saying? More importantly, *how* did I know all this?!

The next thing I knew, Sameer had opened her bag, found my notebook and tossed it to me.

Sanchi, her face tomato red, didn't say anything. I tried to smile at her to say it was fine, but she gave me an ice-cold glare. I just shrugged and pretended to be busy reading.

'How did you know that, Janya?' Sameer asked me after the period had ended.

I shrugged. I was wondering the same damn thing.

Even after class ended, I still could not think properly. I *did* say all that. It *was* me. I said it. Just like what happened after soccer. *I*, Janya, was the one who spoke all that nonsense. What if it wasn't actually bullcrap? What if it actually made sense? After all, Sanchi didn't explain or protest after Sameer found the book.

It was our National Civics class—one of my favourites—but I still couldn't concentrate. I could hear what Mrs. Jain was saying—the sound was going into my ears, but it wasn't entering my brain. Her words took a detour and came out from my other ear.

What the hell was going on?

Lie to Me 9

I wasn't going for soccer today because my knee was still bruised...it couldn't handle running after a ball. So I was stuck alone at home, left to ponder over the strange happenings that had been taking place in my unusually interesting life over the past two weeks. When I couldn't stand the ear-piercing silence anymore, I turned on the TV and began channel-surfing.

Now I'm pretty sure all of us have succumbed to the monotony of channel-surfing many times in our lifetimes, but even after going through the millions of channels that are around these days, you usually don't find anything worth watching. Ironic, because TV was invented for the entertainment of the masses.

Suprisingly, a seemingly interesting movie made me stop pressing the forward button on the remote. And I hadn't seen it before, either. Or heard of it. It wasn't any of the Spiderman, Superman or Batman stuff, but it had the same premise. A man had discovered he had special powers and was trying to come to terms with it. It sure could be disconcerting when the unexplained was happening, not just around you, but *to* you. I felt for him. Bah. It must be the heat...I was empathising with fictional characters.

Wait a minute...*BAM!* Sparks flew inside my brain and you could have seen a light bulb above my head, blinking.

I had put two and two together, finally (despite being terrible at Math).

I rushed to the phone and called Sheila, the irritating next-door neighbour I was earlier forced to play with by Dad for the sake of my non-existent social life. She was the only option at the moment, I thought.

'Sheila, thank you for coming,' I told her as she made her way into the house.

'Oh, no. It's totally fine. I was just listening to music. Nothing big.'

'Oh. Okay.'

'So, what happened?'

'Okay. Come with me.'

I led her to the closet in my room. *I can do this,* I told myself. I could trust her with the astounding information. I mean, who else could I test this crap out with? Dad? Hell, no. I don't have any other friends (forever alone, anyone?). Sheila was my last resort.

'Uh...why are we here? Do you want to show me your new shoes?' she asked. 'Hey, cute top.'

I have a HUGE closet. Well, it's not really a closet for clothes; it has stuff that I don't know where to keep—like door knobs, etc. Actually, it used to be a powder room which was attached to my room. We had no idea what a powder room was, so Dad converted it into a store-room where I could put the 'rubbish' (that's what he called it; to me, it was treasure) I had collected over the years. (I had a lot of such precious items, trust me. A *lot.*)

'First, you have to promise me you won't tell anyone,' I said, in a suddenly intense voice that shocked even me.

'What? Oh, sure.'

'Look here, Sheila. *Focus,*' I said, starting to get a bit annoyed. I wasn't a patient person.

'Okay,' she said, looking right into my eyes with no idea what was going on.

'Now, tell me a lie,' I said.

'What do you mean?' She sat down on the carpet.

'Anything. Just...anything,' I told her.

This was getting nowhere. This could take a whole damn millennium!

'Um...okay. You like cinnamon.'

I felt it. I felt it. I FELT IT! I felt *something* happen. (I didn't like cinnamon at all. I hated it. Blech.) I think I was in a sort of trance or something, because when I regained my senses, Sheila was shaking me very badly.

'Are you okay? Janya, say something! I'm very scared. Oh no. I could go to jail if something happens to you. I would have to wear those stupid outfits! I would have to eat food that's *full* of carbs! Please, don't let that happen to me!' she said, so hysterical that I thought she would wake up the dead.

'I felt it,' I said, when the blurry picture finally became a bit sharper.

'Felt what? What? What did you feel? Oh, thank goodness, you are alive! No striped outfits!' she said, slightly calmer.

I let out a nervous laugh. 'Hey, we aren't here to discuss prison clothes. Let's get back to business, okay?'

'Oh, I see. You are trying to divert my mind, hide something. I see it in your eyes, the fear, the blueness,' she said, trying to talk in a hypnotic tone. She sounded like a whacko.

'Shut up. Tell me another lie.'

'Hmm...okay...how about this...I did not steal your Barbie doll.'

Yes...I felt it again. This time I knew what to expect. I concentrated. Didn't I sound like a geek? Wait, what had she said?

'It was you all along!' I said.

'I'm sorry,' she said, timidly.

'It's okay,' I said, letting it slide. It was just this one time.

Besides, I had more important things to do. I was sure. I could not believe it. But it was true.

I was a human lie detector.

After interrogating Sheila for a while longer, I also discovered that the bigger the lie, the stronger the vibration. For small white lies, just a small tremor. And one other thing. I could not detect my own lies. I wouldn't vibrate when I lied (well, that was a huge relief. I didn't want to be caught vibrating like a freak every time Maya asked me a question). I could detect Oprah Winfrey's lie, probably, but not mine. I could also get the truth out in the open, like I did with the girl at soccer, and Sanchi. But I couldn't tell what the reason was for their lies.

Like, when Sheila was telling me her pointless, totally obvious lies, the BZZT!!! rate was pretty low. But when Sanchi uttered *her* lie, the BZZT!!! rate was off the charts. It seemed more violent, like a little monster was trying to get out of a glass jar.

I thought back to the first time I had this strange feeling. Sanchi had been talking about Zayn, her boyfriend. I bet they had more fights than I could count and all that 'love' stuff she said they both felt for each other was crap.

There was no other explanation. I had gone on the Internet and tried to see if anything like 'internal electric circuit' or 'internal shock' existed, but all I got was a bunch of phone numbers to contact repairmen.

Well, at least I didn't have a disease. I would hate to be the person who discovered a new kind of illness by suffering from it. I wondered who the first person was who got malaria. Poor dude (or dudette).

It seemed really stupid, and there was a huge chance I could be wrong, but my gut told me I was spot on. The girl at soccer had really gotten kicked out of the team, and Sanchi had really kept my Punjabi notebook. My tongue had insisted that she had the notebook in her bag, even when she denied it. And Sameer *did* find it there. But why would Sanchi do that?

So there. I even had proof now that I wasn't crazy.

'Wow. I can't believe it's true. Now I get it.' I was talking to myself, forgetting that someone else was also there in the room besides me.

'Hello? Janya?' she said, trying to bring me back to earth.

'Yeah, I'm here. Oh, Sheila, thank you so much!' I said, hugging her.

'Um...You're welcome?' She sounded totally confused. I wasn't going to tell her. I wasn't going to tell anybody. I wanted it to remain the way it was—top secret. What if she told someone? I couldn't take my chances. And whoever

I said this to would think I was crazy. Which I was, thank you very much, but believing myself to be a human lie detector wasn't part of my craziness. That was a fact.

But there was one thing I didn't get…actually, there were *many* things I didn't get. How did this suddenly happen? And why hadn't it happened before, why now? And why would someone like *me* possess this weird, messed-up superpower all of a sudden?

What was I supposed to do with it? Was I supposed to be like Spiderman or Batman and use my powers to bring good to the world and destroy all the evil forces in the universe? But I had no time for all that…I still had to go to school! What a waste.

Could I use it for my own purposes, or would that be considered exploitation? And could there be an instance when my lie-detecting ability would be proved wrong?

Would this 'superpower' ever go away?

Did I want it to go away?

Was this really happening?

Why So Truthful, World? 10

I entered class the next day, holding on to the straps of my backpack while it was slung on my shoulders. That had been my habit since the sixth grade or something. That was a long time because my habits changed monthly. Like when I used to crack my knuckles. I stopped doing that a few months ago because Dad told me my fingers would fall off. I did not want that.

I couldn't wait to test my lie-detecting powers! What new surprises lay ahead? Would I be able to read minds too? Would I be able to teleport myself? Could I become invisible and sneak up on people?

But I couldn't believe my luck that day. *Why* wasn't anyone lying? If they didn't lie, then how would I detect their lies? No one else's life could ever be as unexciting as mine.

Okay, other than that, the whole day was good. I had fun. Especially during recess. Our fourth period was free so, like everyone else, Sameer and I decided to work on our project. We were halfway through when the bell rang. He went away and I went to the classroom to get my food.

It was then that I noticed I hadn't got my lunch. Oh CRAP! I couldn't believe Dad had done this to me! ARGH!

'What's wrong?' Sameer had still not left the classroom, which was now empty.

'I forgot to bring my tiffin box,' I said, looking up from my bag.

'Ooh. That's bad,' Sameer was trying to be sympathetic, but I could sense that all he wanted to do was get out of this room and be far away from the crazy person (a.k.a me).

'Uh...'

'Um...you want to come with me?' asked Sameer. OH MY GOD. OH MY DEITY. OH MY SUPERNATURAL BEING. Crap. I couldn't *believe* what he had just told me. Were my ears clogged? What was wrong with me? Maybe my brain was not responding, like the computers in our school.

I just threw him a confused look.

'What?' he demanded, impatiently.

'Okay.' I couldn't really say no. See, if I had said no, the scene would probably have gone like this:

'Um...you want to come with me?' Sameer said.

'No.'

'Hmph. You are one crazily weird girl, I tell you.'

Then he would have turned into a poisonous yellow dragon and swallowed me up in one go. Thankfully, I said yes.

So how was the most exciting recess of my life? I'll tell you alright. Sameer, feeling slightly weird, and I, feeling slightly nervous, rushed down the flight of stairs and went to his table outside. He usually ate with a whole mob of other people. Wow. He was a popular guy.

We joined the crowd and he offered me some of his food.

First, I refused, politely, 'No, thanks.' I was parched and starved, but by some logic, it was always polite to say no first. (I learnt that from adults. The first time anyone offered them food, they said no. Then, when they were asked again, they almost always said, 'Oh yes, yes, sure!' and ate like hogs. That was just the way grown-ups behaved.)

So the next time he offered, I took some of his lunch. I mean, why not? In my opinion, refusing something was rude. And the food was *Sameer's*. I mean, come on. That was one thing I learnt during recess. Never refuse if someone offers very nicely. But not cigarettes. Or atom bombs. I surely wouldn't want to be carrying an atom bomb around everywhere. Never mind. Forget the rule.

I didn't know what to do after I had eaten, though. Should I go away, or should I stay and risk feeling really left out? But if I went away, it would look like I was just there for the food. Sigh. I overanalysed everything.

Sameer was talking to Zayn, Sanchi's boyfriend. He was a big jerk. Zayn, not Sameer. The weird thing about boys was, they could be friends with anyone, mean or nice. They treated everyone the same.

If you thought about us girls, it was not that simple. Actually, it was *very* complicated. Girls were mean. They got jealous of others. And their jealousy could drive them to endless possibilities. Guys hardly made fun of each other. They were more united. It was almost like they didn't feel anything.

By the way, the ASS group (Aditi, Sanchi, and their tail, Smitha) had been ignoring me outright for so long now. Now that was some *serious ignoring power*. But why would I want to think about them when I was having the time of my life with this amazing guy? I threw Sameer a slightly annoyed look after some time, because it seemed like he had forgotten I was alive. And just then, he looked at me, and smiled. It was like the whole world stopped and stared for a while. (How could I be so corny? Ugh.)

After a minute, he was no longer in front of me and reappeared at my side. 'Come on,' he said, indicating that he wanted us to move away from the crowd.

'Uh...I am really sorry for disturbing you and all. I could understand that you were having an intense conversation with Zayn,' I said, trying my best to sound genuinely sorry.

'Are you kidding? I needed an excuse to escape. Even a Math test would have been better than talking to him! Or... maybe not. Thank YOU for saving me. Again. Now I owe you service even after I die. I'll come back and haunt you like a ghost,' joked Sameer.

Note to self—Sameer disliked Math.

'Well, I'll surely be scared. Just don't drop into my bedroom at night like in those *Twilight* books,' I said, trying to be funny.

'Ha, ha, ha.'

He thought that devilish laugh made him sound scary.

After a long, intense conversation about our mutual dislike of Indian television dramas, the possessed bell ended it all.

I looked around while in the queue to go back into the school building, and something caught my eye. It was Aditi and Sanchi, whispering to each other, and glancing at me. What? Were my eyes deceiving me?

Then later on, it was our Math group period. We were supposed to sit in our pre-assigned groups, and my group happened to be Aditi, Sanchi and the Quiet Nosy Leech, Smitha. I felt weird because it was like a silent fight was going on between us.

Didn't everyone have that clingy person in their lives, who followed you around everywhere, heard everything you say, but didn't say anything themselves? And you felt it would be too mean to tell them to get lost. That was what I felt about the Quiet Nosy Leech/Smitha. Story of my life.

So we all sat together in this awkward silence, during Math 'activity' period. The teacher gave us blocks, and we were supposed to make something out of them. I mean, seriously? I loved the idea of acting like kids, but this was just *lame.*

No one started building anything on our table, so I just absent-mindedly picked up some blocks and started joining them. Aditi and Sanchi suddenly began whispering. Instinctively, I knew they were saying something about me.

That Quiet Nosy Leech was trying hard to butt into their conversation and I was trying hard not to say anything.

'So, um, is something wrong, guys?' I just couldn't help myself.

'No,' they replied in unison. BZZT!!! Liars.

Count to 10, I told myself. I just couldn't do it. I just wanted to think. Ugh, pimply feeling. I excused myself to the bathroom, where I planned to spend most of this period. It was the last class of the day, anyway.

Whew, thankfully I didn't have to wait much longer to go home. I was so glad when I reached.

I had just settled down when the phone rang. I picked it up on the second ring. After I heard the voice at the other end, my hands and feet turned cold.

'Heeyyy, Mehak, this is Mandira.'

It seemed like *I* was going to be butting into *this* conversation.

Painful Smiles 11

'Oh, hey,' I said, pretending to be this so-called 'Mehak', wondering if I was doing the right thing.

'Aren't you going to ask me how things went with Ashish? I mean, you were the one who came up with this plan.'

Mehak must be Mandira's gang leader, or something. In other words, she must be Mandira's twisted friend—an octave more evil than her. Wow. Was that even possible?

'Tell me,' I asked.

My brain was going out of control. *I was such a schemer*! 'Well, he's a total fool. Everything is going so well. I just hope we don't get arrested this time. I think I will soon become the manager like I wanted and then all that's left to be done will be...' she was interrupted.

'Oh, no! Someone is coming! I have to go! Talk to you later!'

All I heard after that was *beep beep beep*.

But what did she say...arrested? Mandira and Mehak were arrested? What was going on?

After trying in vain to come up with an explanation—and immersing myself in a marathon of *The Simpsons*, popcorn and homework (not really)—it was 9 p.m. Where was Dad? Suddenly, the bell rang. I sprinted to the upstairs balcony, and peeped out to see who was outside the door. It was him. He had brought a guest. *An unwelcome guest.*

Okay, okay. Calm down, girl. I told myself. This was it. This was the time to prove that I was a real devil from hell with supernatural powers. (Sort of. I had no idea what else I could do. I mean, I couldn't do any of the awesome stuff the world-famous superheroes did so easily. I could only detect people's lies and occasionally correct them, the results of which may or may not result in mayhem. How unexciting.)

I ran to open the door, trying not to look as frazzled as I was.

'Hey, Janya! How was your day?' Dad put on his cheerful act.

'Oh, it was fine, Dad,' I said.

I dared myself to look at the witch, who was wearing a *hideous* dress. Okay, it was actually not that bad, but I hated her, hence I hated anything associated with her. 'Oh, and this is Mandira.' As if I didn't already know. 'Mandira, this is Janya.'

'Hello.' A condescending croak. Ugh, I really hated the living crap out of her.

'I invited Mandira to our house tonight. Isn't that great?'

I returned Dad's phoney smile.

Then both of them walked into the house, Mandira checking out the surroundings with her greedy, beady eyes.

'You have a very pretty house,' she said, as she sat down on the sofa.

I turned and started walking to my room, but Dad said, 'Janya, please give Mandira some company while I make tea.'

Really, Dad? *Really?*

I quietly went and took a seat on the couch adjacent to hers. I wasn't in the mood for conversation, especially with *her*! Anyway, Dad hadn't said anything about actually talking. I just had to sit next to her so she wouldn't be alone.

But she obviously wasn't satisfied with just that and wanted to engage in small talk.

'So, which class are you in?'

'Eighth.'

'That's not such a big class. I thought you would be older.'

'Hmmm.'

'So, you have friends?' she asked.

'Dad, how long is the tea going to take?'

'Just a minute,' Dad replied.

'Do you like dancing?' She was unstoppable.

'No.'

'Well, you know, I had represented my school in the national dance competiton when I was your age. I won a lot of prizes.'

BZZT!!!!

'Really? I thought you were suspended in 8th grade because you tried to attack a teacher.'

That did it. She was flabbergasted.

Well, I was glad that conversation came to a halt because Dad had come from the kitchen carrying two cups of tea, and one coffee. *Great*. I would be stuck here for even longer.

'Oh please, no sugar for me. I'm on a non-fat diet.'

BZZT!!! She had just eaten a chocolate sundae yesterday. I guess she just wanted to seem *elegant* or something. But I kept myself from saying it out loud because Dad was there.

'Oh. Well, Janya and I never miss putting sugar in our drinks, do we, Janya?'

'Of course not, *Daddy*.'

'Janya and I were just talking about my school days. Did you know that I topped my class in 11th grade?'

BZZT!!! I covered my mouth. If my psychobabble started now, I would get an earful from Dad. Well, this was going to be difficult.

'Oh, that's wonderful,' Dad said, pleased. Then he looked at me, confused. 'Are you okay, Janya?'

I gave him a thumbs-up, my mouth twisted into a painful, fake smile.

'Hmmm, I don't think she looks very well. Do you want me to give her a quick check-up? I am an expert in Biology.'

BZZT!!! She knew less about Biology than I did.

'Okay.' said Dad.

She sat next to me and took my hand. I'm sure she didn't know what the hell she was doing; she just wanted to impress my father and seem knowledgeable. She really had no limits.

'Well, I think she is a bit dehydrated. And she should watch her weight too...perhaps some more exercise, I suppose.'

Oh, *hell no.* She didn't just comment about my weight! 'I'll just go drink some water.' I said, and got up. While walking to the kitchen, I made sure that I stepped on her foot. *Hard*.

'Ow!'

'Oh my, I am so sorry, Mandira auntie!'

'*Auntie?*' She sounded highly insulted and immediately checked her reflection on the glass table.

I'd had enough of her manipulative talk. And I was worried I would *actually* fall ill, what with all the pathetic lies floating around the room. When I heard she was getting up to go, I was so relieved.

'Well, I think Janya and I are going to get along really well!' Without a doubt, there was a BZZT!!!

And finally, the hurricane was gone.

~

I woke up and stared at the white ceiling. I looked to my right, at the clock. I sighed. It was 7 a.m. Late again. Would this morning get any better?

I shot out of bed, took my Monday uniform out of the closet, and then followed the same hurried routine as always. I couldn't believe it, but I longed to organise my day better. I was so sick of hurrying up for school. Ironically, today was going to be a really slow day. Events of the previous night were still on my mind.

Once I reached, I was greeted by the one and only, Maya a.k.a. the Great Boasting Butthead.

'Hey, Janya!' said the Great Boasting Butthead. I mean, you could just tell she didn't mean it—this cheery act.

'Uh, hi,' I said to the ground, looking at my small feet. Why did I have such phoney people around me all the time?

'How are you, my girl?' She put her arm around me. *Get it off! Get it off!* My brain screamed as if a tarantula was around my neck (though I kind of like spiders. Creepy, I know).

'Uh, good,' I said, confused by her friendliness. Everyone, really, *everyone,* knew (even the teachers) that Maya and I were huge enemends. She must have been trying to extract information out of me! But what information? I didn't have anything to tell. I hardly knew any secrets about anyone.

'I am feeling amazing today!' Maya exclaimed. I was still trying to get her arm off me. She really didn't have to put on this euphoric act; I could see right through it. Who did she think she was fooling?

After 18 seconds of perfect silence (we were walking to the school building, which is precisely 43 steps from the gate where Dad drops me), Maya spoke.

'Um, Janya, I have to ask you something very important.'

Oh my god. Did she know about my lie-detecting powers? But I was sure no one could have found out. I didn't even visibly shudder whenever the BZZT!!!s had happened, if that's what she had noticed. I didn't reply. She may have thought that was an indication to go ahead and say whatever she wanted but I really didn't care. When you didn't reply, it made you look a bit cooler. I don't know why.

As soon as she resumed talking, it turned out that I DID care. 'Is there something going on between you and Sameer?'

Semi-useful Superpower 12

'*Whaaaat?*' I exaggerated my tone. Did she think Sameer was my *boyfriend?* Hell, that would happen only in my wildest dreams.

'Like...you know...,' Maya said, and then we saw our dreary Art teacher staring daggers at us like we were breaking some kind of law that could put us in jail. Seriously. She had such a *fearsome* stare that anyone, even Salman Khan in his brawniest role ever, would get scared.

'Maya. Come here. Janya. You can go.'

Her voice was out of a military school. It wasn't even a voice. The word 'voice' refers to something sensitive. There was nothing sensitive about her. 'Noise' would sum up her style of speaking better. She had these black bags under her eyes and wore a pink *salwar kameez.* Pink! Seriously? The lady would look good in black, nothing else. But I was so happy she had taken Maya away.

It was a Wednesday, and fortunately, I had no soccer today. Well, that was a relief. Now that I had gotten (temporarily) rid of Maya, I could concentrate on what she had just said minutes ago. She was so *BAD*! No one could be dumb or insensitive enough to confirm a rumour from the victim! I bet she spread it too. (I could use words worse than 'BAD'. But Dad would always say I should use the nicest words possible to describe people. He said that if I used 'worse words', then I would start hating that person more. Well, I had no idea how it was humanly possible for me to hate Maya more than I already did.)

My mind told me to recall everything she said to me, then analyse it, and make a list of all the things she could possibly have meant.

My mind also told me to change schools.

That's what I was going to do (the first part, not the latter. I didn't want to go to another school. It would totally mess me up. Not that I wasn't messed up already).

Anyway, what Ms. Boasting Butthead said was:

1. Hey Janya! (Then she put her arm around me).

2. How are you, my girl? (Tried to make me feel comfortable.)

3. (Eighteen seconds of silence.)

4. Is there something going on between you and Sameer?

Point-by-point analysis:

1. She never sounded this happy. I was skeptical about her intentions.

2. She never said 'my girl'. NEVER.

3. The silence? She was such a chatterbox that in 18 seconds of free time she would rattle off so much gossip, it would leave her breathless.

4. Did she really think that Sameer was my boyfriend? That was just weird. I *did* kind of like him, but I wasn't going to be his girlfriend. I wasn't girlfriend material. Besides, he didn't like me. I was just his project partner.

Another thing that had never happened before was that Maya sounded so hesitant while speaking all of the above. She was never shy of talking till she had made her point. That was highly uncharacteristic behaviour.

What was wrong with the world? Was I the only victim left for this crap to be inflicted on?

Sameer wouldn't have done anything, I was sure. He probably didn't even know about the alleged rumours. I wondered what would happen once he found out.

I was sure it was Maya. There was no other explanation. She was jealous because I had been assigned a seat next to Sameer and he was my partner in Geography. She did this just to get back at me. How frustrating. I was trying to make a friend—a good friend—and just because he was a boy, people suddenly had a problem. And this Maya, she had just popped out of nowhere to go around spreading lies. Didn't she have more important things to do? This wasn't why God had given us mouths.

The ASSes were being downright mean to me. Granted, I had made Sanchi look like a fool that day in Punjabi class but hey, it was her mistake. Why would she want to destroy my notebook? My lie-detector was only semi-useful, I decided. It didn't tell me the *motive* behind the lie!

~

Sameer and I were supposed to go to the library today in zero period. I was going to try to look my best. But maybe I shouldn't. I should remain myself. ARGH! I was going mental.

That Mandira problem had also planted itself in my brain. There were no recent updates. But I was keeping my ears peeled at all times. Except while in school, I had to focus on my school problems.

I ran to the school building and when I was on the slippery stairs (there was water leaking from the roof just above), a pack of 7th graders were heading my way. I fought my way through the swarm, and won. Whew! Did the students know they were trying to injure a human lie detector?

I decided not to give a crap about the rumour till I knew Sameer had found out.

I wondered if he knew by recess, which was when we had to work on our project. We were walking together, making our way through the hallway to the library. I didn't notice anything weird, just that I could feel eyes on my back as I walked with him. Maybe it was just my overactive imagination.

We didn't really work as much as talk. The Internet wasn't working and it was impossible to compile information we didn't have.

'I guess we just sit here, praying for the page to load,' said Sameer, looking at my face. I swear I must have looked *so* damn ugly at that moment because he quickly looked the other way.

'Yeah, I guess. Hey, is it just me, or were people staring at us?'

He hesitated. His eyes became dull. 'It was probably just you,' he said, and smiled.

I smiled back, not saying a word.

I decided I should probably not let him know about the stupid rumour thing right now.

'Hey, I don't know if this is too personal or anything,' he said, 'but that day, how did you know what Sanchi was going to do with your notebook?'

'Um, I don't know...I guess it just clicked in my brain.'

'But how could you know about the shredder and everything?' He wasn't convinced.

'I guessed.'

'Hm,' he said. 'You know, I'm still not convinced.'

After working for a bit, I asked him if he liked shifting schools so much.

'Well, it's a bit difficult because I have to make new friends wherever I go, and I know that I will have to move from that place too. But it's kind of nice to meet new people.'

'So you like meeting new people and trying out new things?'

'Yeah, I guess.'

BZZT!!!

'You don't. I know. You would rather sit in your room and read something, or play a video game or even do your homework rather than interact with total strangers that you are forced to be friends with because of your mom's profession. You don't like it when your mom gets new projects and you have to leave everything and move again. But you really have no choice.'

Silence. It was a library; I knew that, but still. He was staring at me with his eyes wide. *Crap,* I thought. *What did I do? Now he was going to think I was some kind of a psychic fanatic!*

'Oh no. I'm so, so sorry!' I said, covering my mouth.

He still didn't say anything...he was just sitting there, astonished.

'Okay, how did you know that?' Sameer asked me, when he had found his voice again.

'Um...well. I guessed?' I was so dead. What was I supposed to tell him?

He stared at me some more. I wasn't enjoying his stares now. They were really starting to freak me out. 'Are you some kind of a mind reader? Or do you have some other supernatural powers?'

I let out a nervous giggle. 'No...what are you talking about? That stuff only happens in movies and books.'

'Oh yeah? Then how could you have guessed something about me that I haven't told *anyone*, even my mom?'

'Umm...because I take body language and expression reading classes? It's part of my preparation for becoming a lawyer, you know.' Oh my god, I was *such* a horrendous liar.

'Tell me, or I won't do the project with you. And I'll pretend you don't even exist.'

I just sat there.

'Please tell me, Janya. I need to know how you know this!' he whined.

I smiled, feeling evil.

He gave me another pleading look, but when he saw that I wouldn't budge, he very dramatically turned around and strutted out of the library.

What was I supposed to do now? I decided to find some more material for the project on my own, since obviously *someone* didn't want to help me out.

No way was I going to tell him. I had promised myself I wouldn't tell *anybody. Not a single soul.*

My research for global warming didn't last long, though. Soon enough, I got bored. There was a reason why teachers paired students up…so they could entertain each other if research got too tedious. And there went the bell.

It was my English period, and I really wasn't in the mood to attend it.

So, I decided to skip it. And this time, I was alone. No distraction, no Bourneville eyes. It was better that way. I needed some alone time. Boys were stupid, needy, dumb creatures.

I decided to stay in the library behind a shelf, in hiding. And if Mr. Tiwari managed to find me, I would just pretend I was looking for poems for a recitation contest. Solid alibi, right?

Well, I wasn't destined to be alone. Just as I wasn't destined to do anything I wanted.

Because as I opened an Agatha Christie novel, I heard someone sniffle. At first, I decided to ignore it. I could make out it was coming from someone sitting right behind the shelf I was leaning on. I focused on my book. But then the crying got louder, so I decided to check it out. I crawled across the aisle, like those cops from the CSI series on TV do, and sneaked over to the other row.

At first, it was hard to see. But it turned out to be someone I knew.

Rumours and Revelations 13

It was Maya!

I was astonished. Maya, the Great Boasting Butthead was crying? I thought she believed in the saying: sticks and stones may break my bones but words will never hurt me. I had known her for a pretty long time, but had never seen her cry. Not even once. I approached her. I mean, I wasn't going to just sit there and enjoy listening to her wails. Although that was quite refreshing; I mean, she had done some *pretty bad things,* but that didn't mean I wanted her to be miserable (for too long). 'Maya, what's wrong?' I sat next to her on the floor.

'J-Janya?' she asked, finally showing her blotched face. It was nice to see her face being ugly once in a while. Spoken like a true enemend. 'What a-are you doing out of c-class?'

'No, that doesn't matter. Tell me why you're crying your eyes out!'

'Well…It happened during recess. I didn't know where you were…'

'Tell me!' I said.

'Y-you know Annika, right? Well, we've been such good friends for so long. You know, we even exchanged friendship bands once. I know, it's corny, but she was so nice to me. But I don't know what's happened… she's started to change. I think it's because she has a boyfriend now. I didn't really approve of him, but I didn't say anything. But you know what h-happened today?' Her sobbing rate had slowed down now.

'What?'

'She told me…in-in front of *everyone* that she couldn't be my friend anymore because she was disgusted by how much of a teacher's pet I was. You know why she called me a teacher's pet? I know she's saying all this because I don't have a *boyfriend.* And all the people from class were watching. I ran out of there because I was already so embarrassed and didn't want to break out in tears in front of so many people. So here I am.'

I was astonished. I thought *Maya* was the kind to pull a snobbish stunt like that. And wait, she *didn't* have a boyfriend?

Wow, I had her pegged as a completely different person.

I hugged her. Real tight. I wasn't really a hugger, but I did it anyway. 'You don't need her.'

'People change, don't they?'

'They definitely do.'

'And there's no need for you to go around and get a boyfriend now. That stuff is not for us.'

She laughed.

'Annika was my only friend. I've realised I have been a bit unpleasant to some people. So they would rather not talk to me. It's not like I hate everyone. I just don't like the way they judge me.'

'I don't judge you.' Lie.

'Hey, you didn't answer my question. What are you doing here?'

'Hmmm, well, I just didn't want to attend English.'

'Yeah, it's kind of pointless, isn't it? Learning grammar. Stupid verbs.'

'Agreed,' I said.

'You're a nice friend, you know that, Janya?'

'Thanks, Maya.'

That was the 'friend' part of enemend talking. But I guess she was telling the truth, because I didn't feel a single electric shock.

We made it back to class before the next teacher arrived. I sat and listened to what all the teachers had to say about their various subjects, and quietly went home. I didn't engage in conversation with Sameer because he was pretending I was invisible. I wondered when he would finally get tired of ignoring me because nobody could possibly resist talking to someone as charismatic as me. Hah.

~

I had another soccer class today. It was terrible. First, the teacher was lying about the number of laps of the ground he took everyday (in reality it was one, or sometimes even zero), then about his achievements in sport (he had only won a bronze medal in an insignificant track race; instead, he said he was a national gold medal winner). Why did he lie so much? I guess teachers thought they had to intimidate their students to show their superiority over them.

When the soccer classes were over, and I began the search for Dad in the sea of treadmills and steppers, it was like I was being electrocuted. People were lying about their height, weight and waist size *everywhere*.

'Oh, I'm a size 4. Size 8 is too fat.'

'Fifty kilogrammes. I can't be any less than that, now, can I?'

'Five feet?! That's damn short! I'm at least 5 feet and 4 inches!'

I found Dad (thank goodness) and ordered him to get the hell out of there, or I was pretty sure my heart would stop beating.

~

Sameer seemed a bit disoriented the next day. He looked like he hadn't got much sleep.

'Hey, what's wrong?' I asked him. We were all waiting for our teacher to arrive.

He acknowledged me with a look, but didn't reply.

'Oh, I see you're still playing that game. Why don't you get it? I told you the truth. I just guessed!'

He remained quiet for a moment, hesitated, and then said, 'Oh yeah? How could you know that my mom's projects were the reason why I shifted so much?'

'Um...well.' I was dumbstruck.

'How did you know I was lying?'

I looked away.

'And how did you know the truth? We just met two weeks ago!' he exclaimed. He really, really wanted to know. 'Or do you just want me to assume that you're a stalker who hides behind a bush every night behind my house and looks at every move my family makes?'

'Dude. Shut up.'

'Okay. Sorry.' He said. Wow, he was being nice now.

'Okay well, I guess I *can* tell you.' I said.

'Great!' He said.

'But you must promise me one thing.'

'Damn. Okay, I promise I will do anything you ask me to do.'

Wow, he really *was* serious. But I'm pretty sure he wouldn't be serious after what I said.

'You must write all my Social Studies essays,' for the whole term.' Haha. No way would he agree to *that.* It wasn't such a good bargain.

'I promise you, Janya, that I will write all your Social Studies essays,' he said, without a second thought.

'Really? I know you don't want to. I know you hate writing essays,' I said, hoping he would be lured into my trap.

'I'm pretty sure. You can even write it on paper, and I will sign it.'

I sighed. 'Just don't think I'm crazy, okay?'

'I already think that.'

I gave him my serious face. He could really cross the line sometimes.

'Sorry.'

'I'maliedetector.'

'You're a what?' He seemed confused.

'A lie detector. A person who can detect lies. And I have proof. And I'm not crazy.'

'Hey, I never said you were crazy.'

'Actually, you did, two minutes ago.' I pointed out.

'Okay, so you're a human lie detector. I get it. It makes sense now. Everything does.'

'Wait a second…you actually believe me?' I asked, surprised. I thought I would tell him and he wouldn't believe me and we would joke about it and he would forget what I had said.

'Um, yes.'

'Okay, well, I did *not* expect that,' I said to myself.

Did I do the right thing by telling him? There was a voice in my head that said I shouldn't have told him; he must *definitely* think of me as a freak now.

'So have you told anyone else?' I shook my head.

'What happens when you hear someone lying?' So I was wrong…he wasn't going to let it go.

I explained the whole deal with the vibrations and the revelations. He seemed confused, but I think he got it. He seemed even more excited than me and kept asking me questions. After some time, I was fighting the urge to slap him.

Anyway, the Social Studies period was quite hilarious. Our History teacher was a real bore, and today, the discussion was about our forefathers. Our teacher started telling us a story about her majestic ancestors, and we had nothing better to do than listen to her drone on and on.

'My ancestors were the majestic kings of the Delhi Sultanate.'

I tried to suppress my laughter. Her ancestors were nothing of the sort.

'They ruled and expanded their kingdom, and were particularly known for poaching wild animals such as tigers and lions. They plundered temples and were fearless.'

I didn't know how long I would be able to stop myself from laughing. The only activity they indulged in near temples was a masterful twiddling of thumbs.

After the period was over, I burst into a fit of laughter. Everyone was staring at me like I was nuts.

Sameer asked me, 'Do I need to call up a mental asylum?'

I tried to slow down my guffaws so I could explain it to him. 'It's just that that the teacher was lying the whole time! Not one thing she said was true!'

'Oh.' He smiled.

'Why are people so superficial?' I wondered out loud when I had recovered from my guffawing fit.

The fact was being driven into my skull with every day that passed with my new powers...people could be extremely fake, lying through their perfectly polished teeth about this, that and the other. It was sad how others believed them. It was sad that such people even existed in the world, people who felt the need to lie at every chance they got. It's not like it was such a difficult thing to tell the truth once in a while. I was starting to lose faith in humanity. Was the world completely fake? Was everything I had believed so far a lie?

Maybe I expected too much. Maybe this was how the world was supposed to be—full of superficial, materialistic liars.

~

That day, after Dad picked me up from school, he said he had to go to the office for some important work. According to him, it was *urgent* and would *only take 15 minutes.* But I had known him long enough to understand what that meant. It meant I would have to go to his office and be stuck there for one hour, with boring people saying boring things.

When we reached, he told me to stay in his room while he did his *work.* He disappeared, leaving me with my school bag. *No way* was I going to be stuck there the whole time. I decided to take a walk around the office. After all, I would inherit this company one day.

I roamed around till I found a certain room that struck my interest. 'Mandira Seth, Chief Manager', said the sign on the door. *Oooh.* This was one place I would like to explore. I looked left and right in the hallway, making sure no one was there. This was the perfect opportunity to find out her real motives. I put my ear against the door to check if someone was inside. When I was certain the room was empty, I slowly opened the door and sneaked inside. That moment would have been perfect if the *Pink Panther* theme song was playing in the background. Life would be epic with background music for every situation.

I entered the office. The room wasn't very large, but it wasn't a cubicle or anything. It was airy, with a desk in the corner. Unlike Dad's desk, it was very tidy. I was tempted to check the emails on her computer. I was already doing something I wasn't supposed to…how bad could it get?

I went to her inbox, and the new mail sign was flashing. A new mail…from 'Mehak'. Oh, I remembered her from that phone call I had overheard. I *had* to read it.

Hey Mandy,

So I hope by now you would have finally gotten hold of the documents. Now all that's left for us to do is get a good hacker, so we are able to get the software from Ashish's computer. A year's work is nearly done.

I'm trying to find a hacker who is willing to help for whatever money you have managed to transfer from Kunika's bank account.

Take care,
Mehak.

Wait, what?

Mandira wanted some kind of software that only Dad had access to?

And they had *stolen* from Kunika's bank account? And what documents were they talking about?

What was going on?

Suddenly, I saw the doorknob turn. I had to think fast. Come on, brain cells! I sat down on the chair in front of the desk, with a really innocent look on my face. Email? What email? I didn't know any email.

Someone else entered the room with Mandira—a man.

'So, you'll do the job, then?' Mandira asked. She was standing at the door, and she probably hadn't noticed me yet. Or I had developed a new superpower of invisibility.

'Yes, provided it's legal and I have the permission of the owner of the computer,' the man said. He had a geeky-person voice.

'Yes, there's no such problem.'

I felt such a violent shock…I was this close to falling off the chair I was innocently sitting on. Was this the biggest lie I had ever heard someone tell?

Okay, what was I supposed to say to Mandira now? 'Haha, Mandira, I know all your evil plans now and I'm going to run and tell my *Daddy*'? Oh no, what if Dad returned and found me missing?

After the man had left (not more than 60 seconds had passed since the door opened but to me they felt like an hour), Mandira turned around and saw me, shocked for a second. Then, as any woman living in a civilised society, she put on her 'nice-woman' façade and sashayed her way to me. 'Hey Janya! What brings you here?' She had a smile plastered on her face.

'Well, I just wanted to meet Dad's new chief manager!' Two could play this fake game.

'Oh, well, it is just wonderful to meet you! You are such a good child!'

BZZT!!!

'Aw, thank you. Well, I think I'd better get going or Dad would wonder where I went.'

'Okay then, see you.' She said, visibly relieved to see me go. After I was out of there, I ran like hell until I got to Dad's office.

To my horror, when I opened the door, I found him sitting there.

'What took you so long?' He asked me, his voice grim.

'Um…eh, I had gone to the washroom and there was a huge rush there.' I lied.

'You know I have a bathroom in my office room, Janya, don't you?' He asked, a bit suspicious.

'Yes, but you see, Dad, it wasn't clean. You should ask the janitor to do his job properly.'

'Hmmm, okay, I suppose you're right. I will, thanks, Janya,' Dad said, satisfied.

I know, I know. Hypocrisy and all. But hey, effortless and harmless lies like this weren't so bad. I mean, I definitely wasn't going to tell the truth in this situation. The only harm would be to the poor janitor.

What was I supposed to tell Dad now? I had to do something; I couldn't just sit on this information. I needed a way to tell Dad that Mandira was evil and she planned to steal some important documents from his computer.

I decided to think about it, but I knew I had to act quickly, or else it would be too late.

~

The next day at school, in the first period, Sameer and I were working on our project in the library. After a while, we got bored. And started talking.

After a long conversation about our mutual dislike of teen pop singers (you know who I mean), I blurted out, 'Do you know about the rumours?'

Oh my god, me and my stupid big mouth should both burn in hell.

'No,' he said.

BZZT!!! He lied! Sameer Sinha, Mr. Extremely Cute Guy, had *lied* to me. He *did* know what was going on. Why was he lying?

He *was* lying.

'You do.' The words just poured out. Crap. I covered my mouth before I said some other damaging things.

'No, I don't.' Sameer's eyes were suddenly as wide as saucers. He looked scary. Or was he scared?

'Hello, lie detector here.'

Silence.

'Look, I don't want to talk about it, okay?' he said, anger dancing around in his eyes. But I hadn't said anything that could possibly have upset him. 'I...uh...okay.'

Everything became quiet and then, suddenly, he took off.

I sat there in front of the slothful computer and banged my fists on the desk so hard that they kicked me out of the library.

What was that all about? I had just asked him a question. Our teachers always said there was no harm in asking questions. I guess whoever said that all good things came to an end sooner or later was right. In my case, it happened sooner. What was I supposed to do? I wasn't going to apologise for my actions because I hadn't said or done anything wrong, in my opinion.

He remained quiet all day, and I made no effort to talk to him. Why should I care if he wasn't man enough to say sorry? Walking out on someone was downright *rude*.

What happened after soccer that evening really freaked me out. The game was fine. We played a match but it was so annoying when the coach kept picking on me. 'No, don't stand like this. Stand straight. Yes, like that. No, you aren't in the right position. Bend your right leg a bit. That's totally wrong!'

I mean, give me a break! I had just partly recovered from a hurt knee!

After the dreaded match got over, I made my way inside the building and trudged over to the gym. I opened the glass door and tried to find Dad. There was loud Punjabi music playing (which I liked...NOT), and there were all sorts of people—fat, skinny, tall, and short lying about something or the other. I was BZZT!!! ing like anything. There was someone on the treadmill, while someone else was working on a machine that seemed like an upside-down contraption for lifting weights. But no Dad. Where was he? I decided to get the hell out of there. I glanced at my watch. It was almost 5:30 p.m. but he was nowhere to be seen. After I had spent 20 minutes searching, I got out of the air-conditioned gym, dead beat. I sat down on the leather sofa in the lobby, feeling lost, empty, hollow. I had felt like this a few times before. Like that time when I was seven years old and Dad and I were buying groceries. I got caught up in a Barbie book—yes, they sold crazy stuff in grocery stores even *then*—and I didn't notice that Dad had moved away from where we were. After I found out that Barbie had busted the bad guys—like she always did—I closed the book, only to find that I was all alone in the aisle. I searched for Dad, on the verge of crying. I finally found him at the checkout counter. Yes, he could be a bit forgetful sometimes.

Like that time, I really, really felt like crying now. This was pathetic. I shouldn't cry. I never cry. I decided to divert my mind. I picked up a fashion magazine that was lying on the glass table in front of me, and started flipping through it. I had no idea what I was going to do next.

How could he *forget* me? Did he not notice? I finally put the magazine down and just stared at my orange and blue sports shoes. I felt my eyes well up with tears, and I was soon silently lamenting my fate (I could use the word 'cry', but it sounds childish). I was so damn sick of everything. First, the stupid rumours, the ASSes making me feel completely isolated, the Mandira stress, the Sameer thing and now this. What did I ever do to deserve all this?

It must have been two or three minutes of these depressing thoughts when someone tapped my shoulder. I turned around.

'I knew it was you,' said Sameer, startling me (I was scared to see who it was because the chances of it being Dad were really less). 'What happened, Janya?'

Behind him was his mom. I think. She had the same dark brown hair and there was a definite resemblance. I wiped my tears, but I knew he had seen me crying…I mean, lamenting. Hadn't he suddenly started hating me during recess today? He walked out on me…why, the nerve of that Greek god. And now he was standing right here.

'I'm lost.'

Little did they know I was lost in ways more than one.

Sameer's mom said, 'Don't worry, we will drop you. Come with us.' I hesitated—but not very much—and decided to go with them. I mean, they couldn't do me any harm.

'Okay.'

They escorted me to their fancy, fancy car. I don't know anything about cars, but that car looked *good*.

I took my place in the back with Sameer while his mom got into the driver's seat. It was weird sitting with him, because all he had done at school that day was ignore me.

He was sitting near the opposite window, and we were totally pretending we didn't know each other. Which we didn't, really. Typical outside-school behaviour. I tried to sit as far away from him as possible. I had too much to think about, anyway.

Sameer's mom asked me my address after a few minutes.

'Are you feeling okay now, honey? Don't worry, we'll be there soon.' She was trying to make me feel better.

'Yeah, I'm fine,' I sighed.

What sport do you learn there?' she continued. Sameer didn't seem like he was going to talk. I guess he still hated me for some reason. But I could feel his eyes on me when I was looking out the window of the fancy, fancy car. I was probably imagining it, like I always do.

'Uh...football.'

'Oh, football. Football is a really nice sport, I tell you. During my childhood days, we didn't have as many facilities as you kids have today, and we had to...'

'Mom, not again with the childhood stories,' Sameer wailed. At least he said something. He was being as quiet as an ant (did ants even talk?). His mom was a really talkative person. Now I knew why Sameer could be a bit of a babbler. Heh. Still, I was trying to ignore him.

I sneaked a look and realised he was writing something on a piece of paper. I was desperate to see it because I had a feeling it was for me. But I pretended I didn't notice and kept looking out of the window.

Before I knew it, we were at the end of the road, and I could see my car parked in the garage. Dad was home.

It had taken us at least half an hour to reach my house. Mrs. Sinha had been driving at quite a slow speed because she was talking all the time. And every few minutes during our journey, Sameer had been sinking lower and lower into his car seat. By the time we reached, he looked as though he would soon be underground.

'Okay, we're here, Janya.'

Sameer tried to pass me the note but by then, Mrs. Sinha had opened the door for me so he quickly withdrew.

'Thank you so much, Mrs. Sinha. I would have been lost if you hadn't dropped me,' I told her, deliberately saying nothing to Sameer. I gave him this cold death stare which, I think, he noticed.

I barged into my house to find Dad on the phone, looking worried. 'Janya? Oh, I am so sorry!' He was so relieved to see my face that he dropped his phone and rushed to the doorway to hug me.

'Dad, your phone's broken,' I told him as I was being suffocated.

'I can't believe I forgot about you! Halfway through the drive back, I realised you weren't in the car. I went back, but the receptionist at the stadium office said you had already left. I even called the police and informed them. Thank goodness you are here. Wait a minute! How did you come back?'

'I found a classmate there and his mom dropped me.'

I wasn't going to say *Sameer* dropped me. I don't know. I didn't feel like. I wanted it to remain a secret, you see. But maybe he noticed I said 'his'. *BIG DEAL.*

'I should have at least thanked them for what they did!' Dad exclaimed.

He was so relieved to see me. I felt bad for him because of all the stress he must have gone through. It had been so long since I saw him genuinely happy. He didn't even laugh much now. We did talk and all, but a real sense of happiness was missing. Poor Dad.

'Okay, Dad. I am going to do my homework.'

His smile faded. 'Okay.'

I went to work on Math. Homework was just an excuse. Actually, I was feeling a bit awkward. Dad hadn't ever been so expressive before that day! After dinner, he came to my room.

'Wow, Janya, your room has changed a lot since I last saw it...,' Dad said, sitting on my bed.

'...which is a week, right?' I finished his sentence.

'Right,' Dad said. I heard the guilt in his voice.

After a few moments of silence, I finally asked, 'Dad, what's wrong?'

Would he tell me something about Mandira?

Forever Alone 14

'Nothing. Is anything wrong with you?'

As soon as he said that…BZZT!!! Liar. He had just lied to me. Everyone told lies…I knew that; it was nothing to get so worked up about. Even Gandhi or Rama must have lied at least once in their life. But Dad? Really? Wow. I didn't expect this from him. AGAIN.

'Really. Dad. I know something is going on.'

Of course he wasn't going to tell me! I was just a kid! *Too small to be perfect!*

'Okay. I'll tell you. I just want to say I'm sorry, Janya. I haven't been behaving like a father lately. I've been very careless. I don't want to be like that anymore. After that time at the grocery store, I promised myself I would be a better person. But with my business going down the drain, I've been so tied up. Now I swear I'll be a better Dad and never ignore you.

'I don't want you to think I'm being distant. Things have not been going well since your mom...passed away. I have been a mess. But I'm so proud of you because of the amazing person you've grown into. I'm just sorry for how I behaved, and I'll try my best to smile more.' Dad's voice was shaking. I hadn't expected to hear all this from him.

'Dad...it's okay.' My eyes were welling up too. I knew it was a cliché and everything, but hey, this *was* a family moment. It didn't happen very often and, very importantly, there was no BZZT!!! while he said all this. I was very happy with what he had told me. But he said nothing about Mandira!

I didn't want to spoil the moment, so I didn't mention her.

The next morning was better than usual. Dad was up and about and reading the newspaper. I was totally surprised at this and even more surprised to find my tiffin box on the dining table. I also reached school early. When Dad dropped me off, there wasn't a hint of sleepiness in his eyes and at the gate, he said, 'Have a great day!'

The guard butted in on that rare, pleasant moment by telling us we weren't allowed to park the car in front of the school gate and that he would complain if we did it again. Stupid fellow.

As I walked past the hall, I noticed most of the junior school population was looking at me...and then whispering to each other. I had no idea what to do so I just shrugged and went to class. I guess everyone knew about the rumour now. It's like the clock had stopped ticking and a bomb was going to explode. What was I supposed to do…brainwash everyone?

I had heard a superstition that if your left ear was itching, it meant people were saying bad stuff about you. Maybe it was just my imagination, but I did feel a slight irritation in precisely that ear. I didn't believe in these superstitions, though, they were totally pointless. If someone (like Sheila) told me about them, I would just brush it off.

I was the subject everyone was whispering about, all the time, even when I went to submit my notebook to a teacher in the staff room. I could hear a buzz in the corridor (where many students hung out to miss a few minutes of class) as I walked there. Some girls said, 'Oh really?'I'm glad I didn't hear the others. They should be glad, too. If I had, the hand that was holding my Geography book would have left a clear impression on their faces. I was so angry. I didn't like being the centre of attention. Most of the time, it was because of something bad. Even though I looked calm on the outside, I was going through a breakdown. Everything was falling apart, and I could do nothing to stop it. Maya must have said something to someone, who passed it on to someone else, and so on. That was how the grapevine worked. Bad news spread like wildfire. *Why* was Maya jealous? Because of my friendship with a guy? No one should get jealous for such a silly thing! But Maya had to, of course. I thought she was nice. I thought she had changed.

I was on my way back from the staff room, ignoring all the 8th and 7th grade glares I was getting. Why did everyone have to go to the washroom all the time? That too, not alone. After recess, Maya came up to me and asked, '*Yaar*, can you come to the washroom with me?'

I refused, of course. You don't go to a washroom with someone else. I didn't want to gossip and wait while she admired her utter ugliness in the mirror. That was an understatement. She, and the other girls who made these 'washroom clubs', were not just ugly. They looked like the walking dead, making themselves look even less alive by doing up their hair again and again and applying pound after pound of lip gloss.

That day I had what felt like the worst four classes of my life. After I ate my lunch, I just roamed around, waiting for the dreadful recess to end. Everyone else was having the time of their lives, I was sure. I didn't know what they found so thrilling about standing around in groups and talking to others. How could that be even remotely exciting?

I looked around at the many bunches of students. There was the It Crowd, which totally sucked. There were the Dancers, who seemed like they never studied. They were always skipping classes and dancing, preparing for one competition or the other. Then, there was a bunch of crazy hysterics who kept laughing all the time…no one knew why. There was also a group of nerds/dorks playing a game with their tiffin boxes and rolled up balls of foil. And a group of meanies who were dubbed *Auntyji*s. Then came the funny guys, and after that the semi-popular cool group (where Sameer fitted in). But I didn't want my brain to turn to mush by thinking of him. He still hated me, I had no doubt, even though he had saved me yesterday. We still sat together in class, but without looking at each other, and talking was out of the question. The closest we came to talking today was when I asked him for a pencil sharpener.

But I decided I didn't care what he thought about me. What was the worst he could do? He was such a jerk. Good-for-nothing freak.

Well, that was quite a venting session. With myself.

I just stood in the middle of the ground. I felt like such a loser.

'Hey!' said an enthusiastic voice. I was looking at my feet at that time. I had really huge feet. Godzilla huge.

'Um, hi.' I looked up to see who it was.

It was *him*. No, not god. *Him*. The guy I hated so much. Wasn't it weird how just a few seconds ago I was thinking about how much I hated him and now we were actually *talking*? I thought he was ignoring me. Why was he talking to me? Guys were weird. And confusing.

'What are you doing here all alone? Aren't you supposed to be with your friends in the It Crowd?' he asked. So we were on talking terms now, just because he felt like it? Or maybe he pitied me. I didn't want his pity.

I still couldn't bring myself to meet his eyes. I was trying to make it look as if I wasn't talking to him, keeping my distance. I think he noticed.

I chuckled. 'And aren't you supposed to be in your Awesome Guys Group?'

'Awesome Guys Group. Funky name.'

Did he never feel sad in his life? Had he forgotten everything? Had he forgotten that we weren't supposed to talk? God only knew what other rumours would follow this conversation of ours. Maybe he was *acting* as if he had forgotten everything. He hadn't even apologised for walking out on me earlier. Should I even be talking to him? What if *he* had spread the rumours?

What was I thinking? He wasn't the type.

'Funky. If you ever say that word again, I swear, I'll slaughter you.'

'Funky monkey!'

He started telling me something, but I was too busy noticing the stares that were fixed on us. It was unsettling. Why hadn't I noticed this before?

What was *wrong* with me? I never used to care what others thought about me. Another voice in my head said, 'Don't let this guy destroy your life.' Was I supposed to act mean or friendly?

I noticed that Sameer had also stopped talking. Even he was staring at me.

'What?' I asked, defensively.

'Huh? I was telling you about the Geography project… what the other kids are doing. They've even printed out pictures. We need to do that too, soon. What's wrong with you? Why are you so...unattentive?'

'Inattentive,' I corrected him. 'I...I gotta go...,' I said, and turned and walked away.

I knew that was rude, but I didn't want to talk to him while being stared at by a whole mob. And he had done the same to me the day before. I wouldn't apologise either. Tit for tat. I ran to the girls' room, ignoring the school prefect who was shouting at me to stay out of the school building.

I didn't know what to do. I stayed there till the bell rang, trying to absorb everything. It was Art. Sameer and I always used to have a ball sitting on the last seat and making fun of our Art teacher. But today, when I came back to class after making my best effort to look normal, I found him sitting with Dev.

Why should I even care? He was just my project partner. That's it. It wasn't like we were friends or something.

Everyone knew it was weird for a girl to have a friend who was a boy. Society *was* like that. It couldn't be changed. Ugh. I sounded like a teacher. Hmmph.

It wasn't my fault. It wasn't my fault that even though I was extremely friendly with everyone, no girl liked me. How did it make a difference if I talked to a boy or a girl? I hardly spoke to anyone in school these days, anyway. The ASSes had been ignoring me for so long. I still didn't know why. A fuse had probably gone off in their heads.

'Good morning, sir.' That dull monotone. There was a substitute teacher for Art. Great. So I was now supposed to sit alone and sulk in my loneliness. Why didn't I bring a book to read?

'Meh,' he gestured at us to sit down.

For the first time in my life, I felt what it was like to actually have no one with you, no one to support you. It was terrible. It felt like my whole world had ended, and there was practically nothing I could do to save myself. And the worst thing was, I didn't even know *why* my friends were ignoring me, especially Aditi and Sanchi. I used to be such good friends with them and then *bam,* one day they decided to act like I didn't even exist.

That wasn't fair. I bet they didn't know what it felt like to be isolated. They were so popular; they always had someone flocking around them. Why didn't anybody care for me?

I decided I had to save myself. I started coughing a lot, and got myself excused to go to the doctor's room. While I went to the door, coughing and whooping, I saw Sameer roll his eyes at me. I looked the other way. I *wasn't* going to the doctor's room. That would be lame. She would give me some useless medicine. I was going somewhere I could think in peace. That turned out to be the girls' room. It was a safe haven where I could escape from the world. I went inside the washroom and locked myself up in the second stall from the left. Think, think, think. When you have a problem, think, think, think.

That sounded vaguely familiar. I tried to think. But I just *couldn't*! I just could not concentrate! I had just *skipped* a class to give myself time to think. And now I couldn't! How could a person *not* think? Before a test, our teachers used to tell us to clear our minds and all that crap and I could never do that. Sigh, I thought of the last time I had skipped a class. I had skipped class a couple of times now. Maybe I was becoming one of those uncontrollable rebels that adults tell us to steer clear of.

I sat on the closed toilet seat, trying to gather my scattered thoughts. I had thought being a lie detector would help me. But no, it was doing quite the opposite—messing things up.

Just then, I heard the bathroom door fly open, and multiple footsteps. Clunk, clunk. They echoed throughout the whole room. I put my legs up so they were not visible, because I was about to do some *serious* eavesdropping. I mean, I *had* eavesdropped a LOT through my life, and I had learnt that eavesdropping could give you a lot of information. That was what I needed.

'Oh, my god. Did you hear the gossip about Janya?' said a voice. Maya!

'Yeah. She is such a loser.' Another nasty voice.

Maya? I had really thought she wasn't the same nasty person after the whole incident with Annika, and our sentimental hugs. But *this?* She was tight with Annika again? Annika, with her you-can't-be-my-friend-if-you-don't-have-a-boyfriend rule! I had actually believed what Maya had told me then. But I guess people like her weren't capable of being anything but disgraceful. The only thing she was good at was being a wretched backstabber. Well, I did feel backstabbed. I felt frontstabbed too. I felt like somebody had stuck a dagger through my heart.

But I guess it was time for me to become strong.

Am I Invisible Too? 15

So she *was* spreading a rumour about me. Wow, she was disgusting. I could say she was evil. But that would be a disgrace to other evil people, and a compliment for her.

'I mean, did you see her confused, innocent face? She was pretending as if she didn't know anything,' the nasty voice chuckled.

A confused person! Me! Most of the time, I knew what was going on!

'She thinks she's so smart, but she isn't fooling anyone.'

Why did they hate me so much? What had I ever done to them? I had never been mean to them...except that time in 1st grade. Maya's friend had stolen my crayons and then I told on her (I'm very protective about my crayons). That wasn't even mean!

'Some people,' Maya said, 'are just drama queens.'

That was it. I couldn't control my feelings anymore. I unlocked the stall door. It was going to get dirty.

They were shocked. Both of them stared at me, scared, as if I was going to kill them. I wouldn't do that, but I sure was going to make them regret being born. It was time to set things straight.

'I may be stupid. I may be innocent. But I am NOT a drama queen.' Anger was bubbling up from my stomach. 'And you have no right to judge other people.'

'Oh yeah?' That was the best friend, speaking for both of them.

'OH YEAH!' I rolled my fists into balls, ready to fight. (I believed in non-violence, but you know, kids around the world had gotten slightly crazy. As had I.)

'Why don't you just go away somewhere with Sameer?'

'What is it with that? Why do you keep adding his name everywhere? What did I *ever* do to you people? What did Sameer ever do?'

'She's hurting my ears,' Maya said, putting her hands over them. 'Let's go.'

With lightning reflexes, I blocked the door before they could reach it.

'Not till you tell me what's going on.'

'What do you mean, what's going on?' asked Maya. Now, wasn't *she* the one pretending to be so innocent with that stupid pug-dog face of hers?

'What are you telling other people?' I asked, frustrated. I was really getting mad. If that other girl wasn't there, I would have smashed Maya's toad face into the mirror.

'I didn't tell anyone anything about you! I swear!'

I did what Dad had taught me to do when I was unable to control my anger. I just spoke calmly, 'Maya, I have only one thing to say to you. I just want to say that you better not make such a mistake again—not only with me, but with anyone else. Because, I'm telling you, you will pay in the end. It isn't nice to start false rumours. How did you think there was something...,' I made air quotes while saying the last word, 'going on between Sameer and me? We are just project partners. What made you think anything else?'

I was totally lying. We were not *just* project partners.

'Because you...you two were always together...,' Maya shivered. I don't know why, but I think I felt a slight buzz inside of me. It was probably nothing, only my own anger.

It wasn't every day that someone was scared of me. I enjoyed the moment, trying to suppress an evil smile (I, too, had an evil side).

'Always? Huh? Always? Name all the times,' I said, channelling my inner bully, who had been silent for a long time. I hardly had anyone to bully.

'Well...in recess...before English...uh...,' Maya stammered.

'Well, you certainly *enjoy* your time with him!' Annika interrupted.

I let out a bitter laugh. 'How funny. So what if I enjoy being with him? And anyways, Maya, you just named *two* situations. Meeting a guy two times doesn't mean he's your boyfriend, okay? And besides, we are too young to have boyfriends! That crap is for 17-year-olds!'

I was starting to sound like a teacher. Apparently *everyone* (me too) in the 7th and 8th grades was going out with someone, according to Maya.

'I know you guys have so much free time that you start making up stories. Stories that may hurt people!'

'Uh...,' Maya sounded freaked out.

I didn't think they understood anything. Maybe she was too scared to think. Maybe she couldn't ever think straight again. Well, at least she was scared of *me*.

'I won't complain to any teacher. Now you must tell everyone that Sameer and I aren't together anymore,' I said, feeling proud of myself.

'I will,' she said, shaking like a Chihuahua before scurrying out of the bathroom with Annika.

I was alone now. I leaned against the freezing glass-tiled walls and began thinking again. Was it a dream? Did everything just get sorted out? Did I just scold Maya? Did she really get scared? I couldn't believe myself; I had done something so...unexpected. It had just happened in a flash! One second I was in the stall, trying to figure out what was going on, and the other, I was outside, trying hard not to kill Maya, shouting softly so that the teachers didn't hear me. (Wait, was shouting softly possible? Now I thought everything was possible after what had I just done.) Five minutes could change everything.

Well, not *everything*, but a lot. Just then, a bell rang. I thought it was a bell from heaven, but it turned out to be for sixth period.

I had just skipped a class. It made me feel like a wanted criminal (although I felt like that quite often now). Sameer was still sitting with Dev, so I decided to sit alone. I didn't really care anymore. Caring would only mean more emotional uproar.

RING! The last bell of the day. All the students rushed out of the room but I was among the last to go. I could see Sameer struggling with his stuff, but when I tried to help, he just brushed me off. He was still avoiding me, and I was still trying to figure out why. It's not like *I* had done anything.

I hopped into Dad's car, which seemed like a secure space. People were not yet done glaring at me. Maya better have told everyone...or else. Or else…nothing. I wasn't a tattletale. I didn't like tattling, but sometimes I just *had* to, because there was no other way. Tattling a *bit* was okay, as long as it didn't hurt those who weren't to blame.

I had just thought of something cool. There was no humour in rumour.

'Hey.'

I couldn't stop thinking about it…what *was* the reason Sameer was ignoring me? I really had no idea!

'Hi, Janya...'

'Hey. Dad.' I paid attention to him just for a moment.

It *seemed* like my crush on Sameer had started to wear off. I mean, he was kind of a D-Bag.

I was in the middle of Stage Three and Four of the Crush Cycle. Soon I would be at Stage Five. Sigh.

I couldn't decide whether to tell Dad about Mandira or not. I needed to tell him in such a way that he would believe me. I didn't want him to think I was some kind of a nutjob. 'So, Dad, how are things going with the company?' I asked him. I had to be very subtle.

He gave me this strange look. Then he said, 'Um, okay, I guess.' After a moment, he added, 'Why the sudden interest, Janya?'

'Um, well, because I was thinking about it and I think that I would also like to run a company that does your kind of work when I grow up. It sounds pretty cool.'

'Maybe I should skip going to office today, and tell you a bit more about my profession,' he sounded happy and surprised. Well, this was the only way. He took out his BlackBerry, and dialled his secretary. They had demoted Kunika to being a secretary. Wow. I wondered if she had any idea about the money being deducted from her bank account.

'Hi, Kunika. Yes, Kunika, I am very well. Listen, about that meeting with Mr. Arun. Can you squeeze it into tomorrow's schedule? Oh, I'll be very busy tomorrow? Please try, okay? It'll...'

'So, Dad, what kind of software do you use? Is it something special? There must be a reason why your company tends to stand out from the others.' I was acting like a nosy reporter.

'Oh!' He sounded even more surprised. 'As a matter of fact, yes, Janya, we do have a secret programme, which is yet to be patented. It helps us to work in a different manner than the other companies, and probably the reason why you think we stand out.' He seemed flattered. Sometimes flattery *was* the solution.

Okay. This was it. I was telling him. If I didn't tell him now, it would never happen.

'Dad...there's this woman, Mandira. I know I've met her only a few times, but I have this inkling about her... about her not being who she seems to you. I don't think she's a good person. I heard her say something... and I think she wants that secret programme,' I said, aware I was making no sense whatsoever.

'What?' Dad looked at me, and pulled over the car on the side of the highway.

'Well, one day she—' I was interrupted.

'Oh, hold on. I have a phone call.'

That sentence really did it for me. I couldn't be patient anymore. I was going to blow my top...all the steam would rush out like a volcano, spewing anger everywhere. How could he do this to me? Why did he never have time for me? Just a second before, he was so nice, and all of a sudden I felt so alienated! Why did this always happen to me? My life was just so messed up. There was the Sameer problem which I seriously had *no* solution for. Then Aditi and Sanchi—oh, you know what? Forget them! I didn't *care* about them anymore. They were freaks who wanted to kill me and then eat my soul. I wonder what I had seen in them that made them worthy enough to be my 'besties' or for that matter, even my *friends*. They didn't deserve to be.

Anyway, school was out for four days because of some seminar half the teachers had to attend. Thank goodness I didn't have to face my school problems any time soon. The only thing that mattered right now was Dad. And I needed to save him before it was too late.

Dad had stopped the car by the side of a flyover, and was outside on the narrow path, talking on the phone. I was so, so angry. He *never* let me complete my sentences, and *never* heard any story of mine fully. He always responded with, 'Mmhm. Mmhm.' Ugh! He was so frustrating. I wanted to crawl in a hole, sleep for 20 years like Rip Van Winkle and wake up and tell him 'I told you so!' when everything I was afraid of had happened. I was tired of waiting. I was tired of being ignored.

AUGH! I got out of the passenger seat and slammed the car door shut. Dad had been outside for 10 minutes now. I marched up to him, snatched the phone out of his hand and threw it off the edge, into the eternal dump of slums below.

In Restless Dreams 16

It was one of those slow-motion sequences. With opera music playing in the background. All in high definition. Dad stared daggers at me as if I was psychotic. But he was mistaken. *He* was the psycho. 'What did you do?' he shouted.

It started sinking in. I had thrown my father's super expensive phone off a flyover. What would he say? Big deal. I didn't feel any guilt. I felt as rebellious as Harry Potter when he formed Dumbledore's Army. (Of course, I would trade my superpower to become a witch any day. I mean, it would be awesome to just paralyse anyone when they made me mad, and then erase their memory.)

I smiled to myself when Dad scolded me and told me to get into the car. I cherished each moment of the car ride and the angry glares on the way home. These were quite enchanting moments. Wow. I felt so free. Sadly, the freedom lasted only till I got home.

'This is the *limit,* Janya. You have crossed it, actually. Stop interfering in my business! You don't need to care about Mandira! That is *my LIFE!*'

I got angry again. I stomped to my bedroom and locked the door. Dad pounded on it for a while, but I kept it shut. I was *not* going to open it for a long, long time. I just realised I had thrown my first stereotypical teenage tantrum. Wow, I was good at this.

I had not cried for a long time and I wasn't going to start now. I wasn't going to cry because of someone who didn't deserve my tears. I was just trying to *help* him. How could he just push me away?

It was only when I checked my little wristwatch that I realised it was way past my bedtime.

I couldn't sleep. I lay in bed for some time, going over the events of the week. It was way too much. Circumstances were completely different a week ago.

Then I started counting sheep. Wasn't that stupid? But then, why was this exercise so popular? It must work! I conjured up a green field and a cute little white picket fence in my mind and dreamt of fuzzy little sheep jumping over the fence. I must have been on 73 when sleep began taking hold of me. Everything started getting blurry. I must have drifted off, because the next thing I saw could only be a horrible dream.

Wow, I would rather have gone to school than face a problem like that.

I saw myself as a small sheep, with another well-built sheep (well-built sheep, seriously, Janya?) who was trying to rip off my soft wool. Then, two more female sheep started trying the same thing. The only difference was that they were less vicious. I tried to defend myself, but I was cornered. I saw a male sheep coming my way. My saviour, I thought. But as he got closer, he turned into a ghoulish monster like the others and I felt like I was getting smaller and smaller. I tried to scream, but no sound came out of my mouth.

I woke up in a pool of sweat. It had only been two hours, but it seemed like several. I couldn't even imagine trying to sleep again so I just lay on my bed like a corpse and got lost in my thoughts.

I couldn't expect everything to be the way I wanted. I couldn't expect everything to happen all by itself. I had to do *something* to change my horrible life. I couldn't just sit here forever. I would have to face the world sooner or later. So why not now? I was going to face my problems like I had dealt with Maya (ex*cept* not with so much quiet shouting). It was 3 a.m. I looked out of the window. Everything seemed so tranquil. Everything…except me.

I opened the door to the dark hallway. This was step one. Conversation.

Dad's room was next to mine. I tried peering in through the keyhole but it was pitch-dark. He must have slept off. It's not like he would stay awake worrying for me. I was just a burden to him. I felt a lump in my throat and tried to swallow.

'Janya, you haven't cried for a long, long time,' I said to myself. I wasn't going to start now.

I opened the door. I had no idea what I was going to do. I just started talking. 'Dad, I don't know if you're asleep or awake, I just want to say something. I'm sorry. I'm sorry for doing the non-Janya-like stuff I've been doing lately. I don't know what has happened, but I've changed too much for me to handle in these past few weeks. Things have not been as good as they used to be at school. So that really turned me off.

'My friends...are not my friends anymore. Things kind of got...messed up at school, and you don't listen to me anymore. I threw your phone away because I wanted your attention. You have more than enough money to buy another one. When you start talking about work, you do it for an hour. I couldn't stand all this anymore.'

Dad still had his back to me on the bed and hadn't changed his position.

I started to walk to the door, when I heard him say, 'Janya, I'm the one who should be sorry. I have been a really horrible person to you for the past 13 years. I didn't even celebrate your birthday properly! I've really messed up. Thank you for making me realise that.'

I was in awe. Did he just say that? He was standing right in front of me now, with bloodshot eyes and hair like a hobo's.

My heart felt like it was going to lurch out of my throat. My toes and fingers felt like I had put them in the freezer for two hours. Was this really happening? 'Dad...,' I had no words apart from that. There were so many things on my mind that I just couldn't form sentences. This didn't happen to me often. So I blurted the first thought that came into my brain.

'That Mandira lady is not nice, Dad. I heard her talking on the phone about how she was going to destroy you. And then…and then I saw this email about her plans…. and then—' I shot off.

'Oh, really?' Dad's tone sounded like he was listening to me but not believing a word I said.

'Yeah, Dad. She's trying to take over your company. She wants some kind of secret software. And then she's going to...'

'No, she isn't, she's doing a good job. Why would she want to steal something?'

BZZT!!!

'She's so responsible and professional and has been telling me to take a break, like I've been thinking for a while! She offered to take over my job in India so that I could resign and become a retired CEO! Then we'll move to Thailand, where I'll buy this really nice house! I'm getting bored of working, anyway.'

There were so many BZZT!!! vibrations that I was having a mini-seizure right there.

'No Dad! What are you...? I don't want to move to Thailand!'

Okay, that was completely random. Moving to *Thailand,* of all the places in the world? Really, Dad? REALLY? Unwilling to continue the conversation anymore, I remained quiet.

'Let's forget about this, just for now, please, Janya, and not spoil the moment, okay?' Dad asked.

'Okay.' I decided to do what he said (for once) and went back to my room, and fell asleep surprisingly quickly.

~

The next day was a bit better, though. Things weren't so weird between Dad and me. I think he had forgotten about the half-awake conversation we had last night…that was a relief. I didn't have to go to school, thank goodness for that, too. But I wondered sometimes if I would be better off going to school than being stuck here, in my very depressing and lonely home.

Dad had to go grocery shopping, and as I loved grocery shopping (because I could randomly get whatever junk food I wanted and Dad would be too busy to notice), I decided to tag along with him. While we were there, some 'very important' person called him (as usual) and he went a little distance away to talk. So I was left alone. Abandoned.

I stood there, in front of the deserted frozen food counter, thinking if I should take the potato Smilies or not. Because I didn't want to get any fatter. I couldn't afford it.

Then I saw someone. *Someone.*

'Hey, Janya.'

I growled, 'What do you want?' without looking up.

'Calm down, little slug,' he said, trying to be funny.

I said nothing, still staring at the glass display of potato wedges.

'What are you here for?' I was curious. I wondered if I sounded rude. Well, I had every reason to be rude to him.

I looked up to see if Dad was returning, but he was far, far away. Great. I would have to keep talking to this douchenozzle.

'Mom needs peas…which happen to be in the frozen food section.'

'Oh.'

I looked horrifying, I realised. I had the worst fuzzy hair. I was wearing my baggiest jeans and one of my insult-emblazoned t-shirts.

'Nice one.' He was looking at it.

I smiled, but it seemed more like a smirk.

Looking the other way, I pretended I didn't know him. When I looked to my right again, he was gone.

Dad came back. He didn't even *apologise*. I guess I just had great expectations.

This was horrible. Horrifyingly horrible, Maya would say. I wondered what was up with her. I wondered if she missed me. Not that I cared. She would probably be backstabbing me a little bit more with her two-faced friend.

Why did Sameer have to go away like that? Did he like being such a drama queen all the time? Was he trying to be like Shahid Kapoor in one of those much-too-dramatic movies? Not even Shahid Kapoor was so melodramatic. I wonder what Shahid would say to me if I ever met him. He would probably start dancing or something. I sighed. My life had the worst timing!

When we got back home, I saw a bouquet of daisies as soon as I opened the door.

Sameer. The first word that came to my mind when I saw them. How nice of him. *That's* why he didn't apologise at the pharmacy. Because he was going to send me *daisies.* How sweet. And he even knew my *address.* Awww.

Suddenly, a worry line emerged on my forehead. What would Dad say?

'Wow, Janya, looks like someone sent you flowers!' said Dad, bending down to pick them up. They were beautiful. How did he know I liked daisies such a lot? Wow. It must have cost a fortune. 'Hey, look, there's a note in it...'

He started opening the folded sheet of paper, but I snatched it from him. I didn't want him to read that! It was mine! It was *personal*! I would be a piece of dead salami if he read it!

Oh, my god. What could be written inside? EEP! I couldn't believe Sameer was being so nice!

I rushed to my room with the note in one hand and the daisies in the other. I unfolded it.

About Turns 17

Hi, Janya.

I guess I need to make things clearer. I don't know if I can say this when we are face to face, so I decided to write to you. Yes, it's the coward's way out but I'm increasingly realising that maybe that's who I am. Annika was my only friend, so when she abandoned me just like that, I felt devastated. But I found a way to make her talk to me…by saying bad things about you. At first I felt good, because I had earned my friend back. But then I realised I was hurting someone else's feelings—yours. And that wasn't fair. I tried convincing Annika that you are a nice person, but she didn't want to cooperate. So I told her I wasn't going to say such mean things about anyone anymore, even if it meant she wasn't going to talk to me.

I just want to apologise for being mean to you. You are a wonderful, supportive girl, who spoke to me even when I was rude, and I really appreciate you for that. I can't wait to see you again. Oh, and when we all return to school, your stupid rumour would probably have become history.

Maya

Maya?

So it wasn't Sameer. Of COURSE it wasn't him. Why would that selfish good-for-nothing twit do anything for me? He wouldn't even admit he was being an ass! HE was acting like he belonged in the ASSes group.

Boy, was I shocked to see a card from her! She must have really changed since last week! It made sense now… kind of. It did seem quite suspicious that Maya was being overfriendly…maybe she wanted something from me. What if this was Maya and Annika's plan? If it was some other person, I would have probably thought they have turned over a new leaf, but Maya? No, I had known her for a long time and this didn't fit her character. The next thing I knew, she would go back to being her usual cold, evil and alienated self.

How could she 'not wait to see me again'? Didn't she hate me since 1st grade, when I had called her 'mean'? Or when her friend stole my 64-pack crayons? We were meant to be sworn enemies! Even the teachers knew we hated each other!

How could she like me? I thought she hated me! I surely hated her! Did she really think I was a wonderful and supportive girl? No one had ever said that to me before, not even Aditi.

Wow. I knew people could change. But not Maya! I didn't even know if she could be included in the category: people. This was probably a trick. I wasn't sure, though. I would find out in some days. Could things really be so different?

I wondered what happened to the Geography project. I couldn't care less.

After days of complete boredom and hours and hours of cartoons and Nicolas Cage action movies which I wasn't even a fan of, I was ready for school. It seemed like the first day after summer holidays all over again.

The day before I went back, I was cleaning out my closet, looking at very old clothes I used to wear when I was six years old. I hadn't discarded them, and now there were so many that I could clothe the whole city!

Then, I saw those old baggy jeans, from That Day at the Grocery Store (that's what I was calling it now). Just as I was throwing them in the 'discard' pile, I saw a tiny piece of paper peek out from one of its back pockets. It seemed like a note.

> *Janya,*
> *I'm really, really sorry. Please forgive me. Those rumour-mongers are real bagheads. I shouldn't have believed them. I don't know what happened. I guess I just got carried away. It'll be very hard for you to forgive me right now—maybe you'll tear up this note the second you finish reading it—but I wanted to try. Can we get back to being friends again?*
> *Your funky monkey,*
> *Sameer*

This must have been what he was writing in the car that day when his mother was dropping me home. He must have slipped it into my jeans' pocket the day we were at the grocery store. That's why he didn't apologise in person. He had written it down. He had *written* an apology for me.

That was the sweetest thing anyone had ever done for me in my whole life. I wasn't much of a mushy gushy person, but I felt my insides melt.

Ironically, a week ago, these people (Maya and Sameer) were backstabbing me and pretending I didn't exist, respectively.

I didn't even need an alarm to wake up the next day. I was up at 6.45 a.m. automatically. Surprising.

My broken-down car stopped working right in front of the entrance. From 'grrrrrrr', the engine started going 'put, put, put' and then it just stopped. The security guard was coming towards us to tell us off again but Dad stepped on the accelerator and mercifully, the car moved and he drove away.

Why didn't he just buy a new car?

Sigh, the same old place. How good would it be if there was no school? We paid to go to school. So, indirectly, we were actually paying to worry, get tense and suffer. Paying to be miserable. Ugh.

I walked into my class. Attendance was being marked. How was I late today? I had woken up early.

I made my way to my seat in the back of the room and plonked my bag down next to You-Know-Who (no, not Voldemort). I was going to play hard-to-get, I had decided. I took out a library book and opened it. I wasn't intending to read.

I hoped my acting wasn't too bad.

'Janya, you're reading the book upside down.'

Aargh. Sameer. I sighed and looked at him. 'I read your note.'

'Oh...,' he looked like he didn't know what to say next.

'Do you understand now? I got confused because of the rumours. It made me act all hostile. I didn't know you were doing the right thing. These stupid people have nothing better to do. They are such losers...,' he proceeded to mutter more expletives and put his hand over his mouth when he realised everything he was saying. 'Did I really just say that?'

'Oh, it's okay. You shouldn't hide things from friends,' I murmured.

'You really think we can still be friends after all this crap?' Sameer looked hopeful.

'Well, sure we can. It's not like we *really* like each other or anything, right?' I laughed, nervously. My instincts were clearly indicating that he didn't like me. I didn't either, not anymore, but I did want to salvage some pride. I was at Stage Five.

He was such a drama queen. I mean 'king'. Was I insulting him? Couldn't do that to my only friend.

'Well, there was a time when I was crazy about you...,' he mumbled. Wait, what?

'You...you *were* crazy about me?' I asked him, trying to sound very contained, when in reality, I was holding back a scream of excitement and frustration. The latter because he said that he *was* crazy about me. Not is, *was.*

Damn, I had never hated past tense more.

'Uh...,' Sameer said, looking at the table. 'Well...yeah. And this is not like I'm asking you out or something, because I think this girlfriend-boyfriend stuff is...'

'Mumbo jumbo?' I suggested.

'Mumbo jumbo,' he agreed with a smile. Suddenly, it vanished. 'You won't tell anyone, right? Oh, please don't tell the teachers. That would be horrible.'

'Oh, Sameer, come on. I'm not crazy. I'm not even boy crazy.' Yeah, right.

'Well, I'm happy I got *that* off my back. I'm glad you're not one of the mean girls who live to gossip for attention.'

I whispered, almost to myself, 'Who would I gossip with, anyway?'

'What do you mean?' Sameer asked. I was going to tell him. Yes, I had to tell somebody. I couldn't live like crap anymore. I deserved better treatment, good advice, and a better life. Besides, he was the only friend (kind of) that I had.

But I doubted Sameer would give me any advice. What would a 13-year-old Greek god advise *me,* the super-complicated girl?

'My friends have deserted me,' I told him the whole ASS situation.

''Awww, come on. You have me.'

'I don't mean to spoil the moment, but do you notice how corny this is?'

'I do.'

'Sameer, what do you think I should do?' There was no harm in asking him. I didn't have anything to lose, anyway.

'Well, Janya, I think you should confront them.' What a very diplomatic, Dr. Phil voice. 'You ask them who they think they are.'

'Are you crazy? Are you out of your mind? I could never have the guts to say that!' I exclaimed.

'Well, you'll have to find your guts. It's the only way. This, or run them over with a train,' Sameer chuckled.

'Trains solve everything, don't they?' I asked, with a sigh. Did I seriously have to confront those two hags? Ew...

'Hey, come on, you're a living, breathing lie detector. Nothing can stand in your way,' Sameer said.

He sounded like he had memorised a self help book. But still, I smiled.

'When are you planning to have the confrontation?' He air-quoted the last word.

'Right now.'

Time for Action 19

I made my way through the narrow gap between the aisles, very, very slowly, like I had recorded what was going to happen, and was now replaying it for closer inspection. Sigh, I was obsessed with technology. I wished I could rewind and fast forward life too.

Aditi, Sanchi and Smitha were sitting near the front of the classroom talking to each other in low voices. Probably gossiping. When they saw me looking at them, their voices faded away.

It all made sense now. I just hoped I wasn't wrong. And even if I was, it wouldn't really affect my non-existent friendship with them.

'Aditi, Sanchi, what's the deal with you guys?' I asked. I was ignoring Smitha because she was never really a friend, just a leech who was stuck to Aditi.

'What...what do you mean, Janya?' asked Sanchi, in her best imitation of an innocent, vulnerable girl. Honey, Broadway is a long way away.

'You people haven't been acting like my friends.' I told them in my best accusatory voice.

'We've always been good friends to you, Janya.' BZZT!!! Aditi said in her most 'I-didn't-do-anything' tone. My name sounded like an expletive on her tongue.

'You didn't defend me from any of the dirty rumours people have been spreading about me. A true friend would do that. Hell, you may even have been spreading the rumours,' I pointed out.

'Oh come on, Janya, everyone knows what really happened! Everyone knows you asked Sameer out because you didn't want him to slip out of your claws, but the poor guy was forced to say yes. He didn't want to break your heart and you started manipulating him. You spread this rumour *yourself,* just to get attention,' Aditi sneered.

BZZT!!! I didn't need my lie-detecting powers to tell me that wasn't true. I could feel hundreds of eyes on my back. The class was silent, waiting for my comeback.

THAT was the story being spread about me? That was the least creative thing anyone could ever have thought of. There was no way in hell or heaven that Maya had done this. I had known Maya for seven years and from my experience, she had the talent to make up far more vicious tales.

'Aditi, everyone knows those rumours are a hoax. I'm not an attention-seeker, unlike *some people,*' I retorted. 'These rumours were spread by people like you three who have nothing more to do to get revenge on a totally unsuspecting person.'

They fell silent. Suddenly, Sanchi stood up, and the whole class gasped like someone was going to be guillotined. She pointed a finger in my face, about two inches from my nose and said, 'Listen, girl. You've already made a complete fool of us. You're the worst friend anyone could have. Let me get this straight. We did not spread *any* rumour about you. You're just doing this to get people to notice you.'

BZZT!!! Of course. Suddenly, a fuse went off in my brain and I spoke in a voice that surprised even me. I moved towards her and she kept backing off, till she was cornered.

'You *did* spread it. You, along with Aditi, whom I used to trust *so much,* and your little minion, Smitha. Now it makes sense. You guys ignored me because you were jealous I had started doing well in school…you thought only you are smart enough. When I stopped making efforts to tag along with you and started hanging out with a specific person, you got your bait. It was you all along. And I thought we used to like each other. Well, now I certainly know *you* don't, and neither do I.'

The weird part was, I didn't even need my lie-detecting powers to know that they were lying. They were like that all along. I had just ignored it.

And I was able to guess the reason they did this, too. Maybe it was always there, in a place in the back of my mind where the right solutions to all the quadratic equations (that I never seemed to get right) were also hidden.

'Hey, Sanchi, weren't *you* the one who forced your boyfriend to go out with you?' someone said from the back of the class. It was Sameer. I knew it was him.

The class was so silent, pure pin-drop silence. Learn something from me, teachers. It remained quiet until *someone* started crying. Then, it was like a fire of new gossip engulfed the room.

I went back to my seat.

'You did a good job out there,' said Sameer.

'Thanks...,' I felt like I was going to burst with happiness.

'So, *they* were the hags who started the rumours.'

'Thanks for the finishing act,' I smiled.

'You know, I really like your eyes,' he said as he was taking out a notebook from his bag.

I think the rare recurrence of the Crush Cycle was going to happen with me. Right now.

Damn, I owed someone an apology.

You know, life was not how *they* portrayed it in books. In many that I've read, the main character always had two best friends who were completely loyal and they visited each others' houses all the time to practice makeovers, paint their nails and talk about boys. Where were they living, *Rainbowfield* or something? My life could *never* be like that.

One problem solved, two to go.

Soon, it was Drama Time, or as it was more commonly known, recess. And no, I was not going to spend it with Sameer. I had some unfinished business to take care of.

She was standing against a brick wall alone, surprisingly, without her *chamchi*, Annika. I guess she had finally broken her friendship with her for good this time. She was nibbling on a sandwich and looking at her shoes.

Should I really do this? Should I go up to her and apologise? I *had* made a huge mistake. What if she slapped me? She was unpredictable.

My feet started moving towards her. I thought of something as I walked. I just realised that when I had accused her in the bathroom and she had said she was innocent, nothing went BZZT!!! She was telling the truth. I guess I was so blinded by my first impression of her that I didn't want to admit it.

'Maya, I'm so, so, sorry.' I said, looking into her eyes. For the first time, I noticed they were brown-black like mine, and they didn't look as cruel as I had thought.

'So you finally found out,' she mumbled to herself, not bothering to look at me.

'Why didn't you tell me it wasn't you?' I asked, still trying to make eye contact.

There was a long, long pause. She was hesitating. Why? Maya Sharma *never* hesitated. 'Because...because you would not have believed me!' Maya had tears in her eyes.

'Yes, I would have believed you.'

'No, you wouldn't have. You automatically suspected it was *me* when you heard the dirty rumour, didn't you?'

'Yeah...'

'That's because we *hate* each other! We aren't supposed to be friends! *Everyone* knows that.'

I put my hand on her shoulder, trying to comfort her (and probably failing). I wasn't really known for comforting people. 'Why do we care what they think? I think you're…pretty nice, actually. Oh, and is what you said about Annika true?'

She looked away for a moment, and then said, 'Well, Annika has been my only friend. I mean, you were always there too, but we have never really gotten along well with each other. After the fight with Annika, I realised how nice you were to me, but I was so used to hanging out with her that I didn't want to let her go. So I bad-mouthed you to get her back on my side. But then, I did realise I was a terrible human being.'

Wow. 'And I think you aren't as bad as my friend said. You are pretty cool, you know, little punk,' she added.

'Did you just say "punk"?' I asked, amazed.

'Yes, I did.'

'Welcome to my family!' I said, giving her the huggiest hug anyone could have ever given. I'm not the hugging kind but when I do, I give some deadly hugs.

Another problem solved. School problems, *nada*. I never thought this was possible. Why couldn't I sort out my life at home this easily?

I was still worried about Dad. Sure, he had ignored that late night talk, and never really discussed Mandira with me anymore. But still, I knew he remembered that conversation. Trust me, it was hard to forget the little things. And the worst part was, he didn't believe his own daughter. I needed proof. Mandira was making him go wherever *she* wanted, like she had a remote control. She tried to impress him by making a fake portfolio, and it worked. I wish I could give him my lie-detecting powers. He sure needed it more than me.

I was scared. Scared that she would have already hacked into Dad's office computer, and taken what she had to get to complete destroying his business. I was scared of being proved right about her.

I returned to that feeling of dread when I thought about our probable move to Thailand. I would have to leave my awesome house, with the picture-laden walls and my bed with the Barbie stickers.

Most importantly, I didn't to want leave my friends (basically, Sameer and Maya. They were way better than those ASSes I knew! I never thought the day would come when I could call Maya something close to a *friend*).

~

Dad dropped me home. He said he had to go for an important meeting.

Oh, no not again.

I had to do this.

Lalita was working in the house, so I went up to her in the kitchen. 'Um. I need to talk to you.'

'Okay, what?'

'I need your help.'

She started walking away.

'Please!' I begged. 'I swear everything will work out just fine this time.'

She looked at me with disapproving eyes.

'Do you want Dad to know about the time you burnt that shirt of his? The red one that he loved so much?'

I had to resort to blackmail. I know, I know. What are you going to do, huh?

She sighed. 'All right. What are you up to now?'

She should've known it involved driving me somewhere. I was now in front of Dad's office building. Awww, I remembered the last time Lalita had driven me here. I was seven years old and addicted to my Nintendo, which had broken, and I wouldn't stop crying. The good old days.

The second the heavily made-up receptionist looked at me and stood up.

'Who are you?'

Oh, what the hell.

'I am your CEO's daughter.'

'What do you want?' I think she couldn't see the resemblance between Dad and me. We didn't look alike at all.

'I want to go to Dad's office. I have to talk to him.'

'There's a board meeting going on.'

'Which floor?' I asked. Lalita was waiting impatiently behind me. She was just praying she wouldn't get fired.

The receptionist sighed. 'Nine.'

'Thank you!' I said, my voice suddenly bright.

'Wait, why do *you* want to go there?'

I think she understood I was up to something. I ran to the elevator. Glancing back, I saw the receptionist chasing after me.

'Come back here, you little twit!' She couldn't even run in her stilettos without stumbling.

'Fat chance, lady!' I called back. I was at the elevator. Oh crap. It had just left.

Plan B! I found my way to the stairs, and ran upstairs as fast as I could without falling. I was doing pretty well.

I panted. Huffing and puffing like an asthma patient without an inhaler. Which floor was I on? Seventh.

Come on, Janya! You can do this! Only two more floors! I could do it. I could do it. I started running again, my intestines hurting a lot and adrenaline coursing through me. I finally found myself in front of a board which said, in big block letters, FLOOR NINE. Ugh, nine. I would never be able to see that number again without feeling tired.

I was in an isolated hall with no windows. I started walking through it, slowly. The door at the end of the corridor was just inches away.

This could change everything. I could do this. This was it.

I took a deep breath.

I opened the door.

Everyone was staring at me. Well, at least I was used to *that* by now.

There was a long conference table with glasses of water arranged in front of every seat. It was a big room, with two ACs, and one side covered with tinted glass. Two people were standing.

One was a fat old man who worked in the company, the other, Dad.

You're Welcome, Universe 20

'Janya, what the heck are you doing here?' Dad asked me, sounding hoarse.

I looked around the room. There weren't many people in the room. I recognised some familiar faces. I saw Kunika, looking wary. Mandira wasn't there.

'Dad, let me do this. Don't stop me, please. Just listen to me!'

He just stared at me. After he composed himself, he said, 'Okay, Janya.'

'Mandira is a traitor. She's a liar. She has been lying to all of you. She was lying about her portfolio, about her previous jobs, and about her intentions in this company.'

'Now, those are some serious accusations. Do you have any proof available to testify against her?' the old man said.

'As a matter of fact, I do. Please, follow me.'

I ushered the old ladies and men out of the room and led them to her office. Dad was with me. While we were walking, he whispered to me, 'Janya, are you sure about this?'

I looked at him. 'Trust me, Dad. Just this once.'

I opened the door. Seemed like no one was inside. I went to her desktop, and *thankfully,* her email opened without any difficulty. (Quite careless for a small-time crook, eh, Mandira?) I showed them the mail that I had seen before, and after Dad read it, he got that look on his face when I did something I wasn't supposed to. Kunika gasped.

'So that's why the bank put a debt notice on my account!' she exclaimed.

Dad's expression changed from surprise to disapproval to anger in a span of five seconds. Then he stormed off, and I followed him (although it was difficult to keep up), along with the other office people after they had read the email.

He was going to his office to check on his files, to make sure they were safe.

To our surprise, there were already people in the office. And they happened to be Mandira and that geeky hacker. They were sitting in front of Dad's computer.

'Mandira?' Dad said.

Mandira froze. Very slowly, she turned her head. 'I can explain,' she said, in a panicky tone.

'Please do.'

'Well, my computer wasn't working, and I had to make the logs, so I decided to use your computer and mail the logs to my computer.'

BZZT!!! Well, that lie was obvious. Also, she wasn't making eye contact and her face had gone completely red. It was a lie… anyone could tell, lie detector or not.

'Oh? Well, I just very conveniently checked your email on your computer and showed your conversations with Mehak to everyone,' I said.

Mandira said, 'Oh come on, Ashish, you can't possibly believe her. She's just a little girl. She's lying! I will do wonders for your company! Just put me in charge and everything will be alright!' Mandira screeched.

BZZT!!! I felt a sharp vibration inside me, and suddenly, one of the neatly arranged glasses on the table shattered into a million pieces. *Whoa.*

'What was that?'

Everyone looked at me.

'I'm not going to spoil your company! I'm not going to do anything illegal! *She* is lying!' Mandira shouted like those crazy politicians on TV when they argue senselessly with each other.

'No, she is lying. Dad, I'm just trying to help you not end up on the streets, okay? She's going to drive the company into the ground! She just wants the money, that's all! She wants some kind of secret software you have, and use it to earn money. '

'I am not any of those things!' BZZT!!! A stronger vibration. Suddenly, the whole glass window broke and there were shards everywhere.

Dad rushed me outside the door. When everyone was huddled together in the hallway, Dad said, 'I believe you, Janya.'

'What? Really?' I said. What was happening? I was right? The fat old man interrupted us, sounding frantic. 'Mr. Ashish, I was just looking through Ms. Mandira's documents a bit more carefully, and they are fake. The stamp is clearly forged. She never was a kindergarten teacher. Oh, and a police investigation of Ms. Kunika's account transactions were just sent to us, which she had ordered a few days ago. It appears to be a Mehak Pandhi who is behind this. You might want to look into it.'

'Oh no, not Mehak!' Mandira exclaimed.

'So you *are* related to Mehak!' the man said. Suddenly, I was the smartest person in the building.

'I...I...!' She started running to the elevator.

Okay, why do girls who know that they have a job involving running wear high heels? High heels won't get you far, honey.

Suddenly the elevator opened, and out came the angry receptionist (she was looking for me, I bet) and bumped into Mandira. When she understood what was going on, she tackled her, and I got to see a catfight, which continued until the old office guy separated them, and got hold of Mandira.This reminded me of the court scene in Shakespeare's *The Merchant of Venice,* with Dad as Antonio, Mandira as Shylock (of course), me as Portia, and that old office dude as Portia's minion.

'Well, everything worked out quite the way I had planned it,' Dad said, (sarcastically, I think), picking up a shard of broken glass. 'What happened? Was there an earthquake?'

'I don't know. Yeah, maybe there *was* an earthquake.' I lied. I knew exactly what had happened. I knew what had happened quite well.

See, when Mandira lied for the second time in front of me, it caused a surprisingly violent version of the vibration I had been getting, probably because I was so desperate to expose her fraudulence and so angry. The shock waves went all the way down to my feet, travelled across the floor and reached the huge glass window, which shattered. The glass broke in the same way. I was touching the table on which it was placed. But still, I couldn't tell him about me being a human lie detector! No one was supposed to know (except Sameer).

And Mandira was just plain evil. She and Mehak just wanted money and were looking for an easy target, and they thought Dad's company was the best place. Mandira pretended to be a very accomplished and capable person in order to get employment in the company, manipulate the CEO (i.e., my father) and get access to a unique computer software, which Dad had been developing and had not yet patented.

But then *I* came along.

'Well, I don't know what happened either, but I'm glad everything worked out fine. I'm sorry I didn't trust you. This may sound weird, but thanks for saving my company.'

What was I supposed to say? You're welcome?

I smiled. 'It's alright, Dad. At least we're not moving to Thailand. And your whatever-software is safe.'

He smiled back.

Reflection

I can't believe how weird and action-packed this past July has been. My life had never been this *happening*. Over just one month, I got a crush on a guy (who I later found out liked me too, when I had stopped crushing on him, but now I just might like him again. I wonder if there was a time when we both liked each other. Wow. I make me sick), gained superpowers, sneaked into a restaurant, set it on fire, got chased with spaghetti in my hair, eavesdropped numerous times, made some enemies, got two new good (hopefully) friends, saved my Dad's company…I had practically *saved the whole world*.

Oh my god. What a boast.

I hope I'm not becoming a Maya. Maya's not a Maya anymore, though. She's risen above her world of hatred. I hope Aditi and Sanchi will do the same one day, but that day probably isn't going to arrive for a long, long time (sadly).

Well, whatever. I'm happy everything turned out fine. In most of the sentences I wrote here, I have used the words 'I' or 'me'. I am so self-centred.

I still wasn't sure how I got these lie-detecting powers. I wasn't sure *why* I had them. Maybe by mistake, maybe someone wanted me to have it. And honestly, deep down inside, I'm kind of grateful to whoever bestowed upon me these powers. It saved me. God knows if I didn't have these powers what would have happened by now. Sure, it made me realise how superficial and unrealistic people are, but it also made me realise the truth about lying. People are insecure. Everyone is scared. That's why they find the need to lie. It made me realise that everyone is human. It's human instinct to lie. We shouldn't lose faith in humanity just because people lie a little bit.

Well, I guess in cases like Mandira's, things are a bit different, but then, such people are just cruel and don't know what to do with their lives. We can only hope for them.

Speaking of Mandira, Dad filed charges against her, and she will be tried in court soon. Most probably, she will be sent to jail for using the company's data for wrongful purposes (maybe while she's there, she can practice her excellent diagnostic skills and think of an exercise regime for my fat self).

Dad and I get along a lot better now. I don't treat him like a stranger anymore, and I feel comfortable talking about school and my social problems (well, most of them, anyway). I realised I missed out on a lot of time with him by thinking that he and I didn't have anything in common. It turns out we both like a lot of the same things.

Sameer is my friend. We sit together, and probably will until the teacher decides to change our seats again (I just hope she doesn't, for a really, really long time). But I usually hang out with Maya during recess.

Maya has changed. If somebody told me that we would be good friends a month ago, I would not be able to stop myself from letting out a rude snort and breaking into laughter. But times have changed.

Then I remembered. I had a confession to make. I rushed to the phone and punched out a number.

'Hello?' a voice answered.

'Hey. It's me,' I said.

'Oh, hey.'

'Um, Maya, since we are now friends, I just wanted to tell you something because I can't live with the secret anymore. It's killing me.'

'What?' she asked, sounding worried.

'I don't like canteen food. It tastes horrible. I never really liked the pizzas or sandwiches they sell there. The only reason I used to eat them was because I didn't want to look like a self-conscious weight-slash-health freak.'

'Welcome to my club. I used to pretend I like it because of Annika.' She sounded like she was grinning.

I smiled into the phone.

Goodbye, pimply situations!